Praise for Gail Giles's work

SHATTERING GLASS:

ALA Quick Pick for Reluctant Young Adult Readers

ALA Best Book for Young Adults

Booklist Top Ten Mystery for Youth

★ "Grimly comic . . . a surefire hit."

—*Kirkus Reviews*, starred review

"Suspenseful, disturbing. . . ."

—*Publishers Weekly*

★ "The pacing is superb and the story's twists are unexpected and disquieting."

—*Booklist*, starred review

DEAD GIRLS DON'T WRITE LETTERS:

ALA Quick Pick for Reluctant Young Adult Readers

"A tightly spun web of intrigue [that] will captivate readers."

—*Columbus Dispatch*

"Another winner."

—*Kirkus Reviews*

Also by Gail Giles

Dead Girls Don't Write Letters

Shattering Glass

Playing in Traffic

GAIL GILES

Simon Pulse
New York London Toronto Sydney

SIMON PULSE
An imprint of Simon & Schuster Children's Publishing Division
1230 Avenue of the Americas, New York, NY 10020

First published in 2004 by Roaring Brook Press, a division of Holtzbrinck Publishing Holdings Limited Partnership, 2004

The text of this book was set in Friz Quadrata.
Manufactured in the United States of America
First Simon Pulse edition March 2006
10 9 8 7 6 5 4 3 2 1
The Library of Congress has cataloged the hardcover edition as follows:
Giles, Gail.
Playing in traffic / Gail Giles.—1st ed.
p. cm.
"A Deborah Brodie book."
Summary: Shy and unremarkable, seventeen-year-old Matt Lathrop is surprised and flattered to find himself singled out for the sexual attentions of the alluring Skye Colby, until he discovers the evil purpose behind her actions.
ISBN 1-59643-005-2 (hc.)
[1. Family problems—Fiction. 2. Interpersonal relations—Fiction. 3. Parent and child—Fiction. 4. Murder—Fiction. 5. High schools—Fiction. 6. Schools—Fiction.]
I. Title.
PZ7.G3923Pl 2004 [Fic]—dc22
2003017829
ISBN-13: 978-1-4169-0926-2 (pbk.)
ISBN-10: 1-4169-0926-5 (pbk.)

Always and always and always
For
Jim Giles and Josh Jakubik,
My heroes

First and foremost, thanks to Scott Treimel for getting me through this one. Your advice and emotional support were invaluable. Thanks to Matt Whitlock for the loan of his name for my main character, though he is not at all like the Matt of my story. And thank you to Megan Whitlock for her advice on the rave, though her mother and I choose to believe the knowledge is secondhand. Thanks to Cathy Atkins, Betty Monthei, Deb Vanasse, and Cynthia Leitich Smith for early reads and manuscript advice. Thanks to the Roaring Brook folks who work so hard on my behalf. And finally, thanks to those wonderful listserv people on YAWriter and adbooks who give of their knowledge and support so graciously.

Playing in Traffic

Skye

I was the ghost of school corridors.

Skye was the devil.

And I was doomed from the day she spoke to me.

—

I was hauling my massive lit text out of my locker when she shimmied alongside me. She bumped me with her hip and shoved her face up so close there was nothing between our lips but breath.

"Hey, I'm Skye." She sort of rolled and her beyond-fantastic butt made contact with mine as she appeared on my other side. "But you know that, don't you?" Walking her black-polished fingernails along my arm, she pursed her lips.

Yes, I knew that. Skye was said to be as darkly dangerous as she was lushly beautiful. Her closeness made me too damn dizzy to see. But I could smell her. Something dense and deep, like massed flowers at a funeral.

"Cat got your tongue?" She teased the tip of her tongue out between her teeth and licked her *come-kissme* lips.

What was up here? I didn't want her attention or the attention she was generating.

"I have to get to class," I muttered. Slapping my locker closed, I scuttled off.

"Not that easy," she sang.

I hoped no one had seen or heard her. I worked hard at being inconspicuous, and as a result, people tended to look straight through me. My looks are unremarkable, and my mind is good enough to make B's and C's and attuned enough not to make A's. It took three weeks for my teachers to learn my name. But they didn't use it much.

I slid into my seat just before the bell. English is not my main thing and now my mind cruised in my pants. I fidgeted and head-tripped during class. Skye Colby. How had she picked me out, and why? I didn't want this. I didn't need it. I gave myself a mental shakedown and tried to refocus on *Heart of Darkness*.

When I returned to my locker, a piece of notebook paper jutted from the air vent. I edged it out and pulled it in front of me, protecting it from prying eyes. Words slashed in something red and slightly sticky. Blood, I thought. Skye was rumored to be a cutter. But it was lipstick.

"Park. 7. You know you want to." Big letters. Diagonally across the lines and invading the margins. I folded it in half, aligning the edges, and then in half again.

Katy

Katy was banging pots in the kitchen when I got home.

"What's up, Katydidn't?"

My dad calls her Katydid. I think that's a flower or a bug in oldfartspeak. But Katy never did what you expected.

"The moon, stars, and taxes," Katy belted back. Sweet little Katy, closing in on her fourteenth birthday, savagely sarcastic, with a voice like a foghorn. As blond and lanky as I'm dark and wiry—we're complete opposites. She's the funniest person I know, and I'm crazy for her. Not in a perv kind of way.

My mom started her business when Katy was three and I was seven. We had a baby-sitter, but she baby-sat the television and I took care of Katy. With no children my age in the neighborhood, hanging with my kid sister was the only fun I had. I taught her to ride her trike, to throw a ball, and later to play endless games of Uno. I put the ointment and the Band-Aids on the skinned knees. I was the go-to guy when she had a nightmare. I let her push me around.

Now our family reminds me of a boardinghouse with three roomers. Katy and me as a unit, Mom, and Dad.

Mom and Dad seem to see as little of each other as they do of us. In case of emergency only.

I think Katy might be a big reason I tend to compartmentalize things. It was always part of my personality. I don't let different foods touch on my plate. I don't multitask. I close one file on the computer before I open another. I don't play music while I study. I have a different spiral for each class. But I started compartmentalizing people when I was about ten. And Katy was the reason.

But, other than that, I keep myself apart from people, don't let myself care, except for Katy. With Katy, I can be—I don't know—not so closed off. But to relax and belong in Katyworld, I have to keep it totally separate.

"Are you going to cook?" I asked Katy. "There's bound to be some leftovers to nuke."

"I'm making couscous."

"Cous you want to?"

She wrinkled her nose at me. "Lame. I'm thinking about vegetarianism."

"I've already thought about it. Against it."

She chucked a wet sponge at me. Katy will never be a ghost.

Skye

I don't know if Skye was late or I was early. But I parked my you-can't-pick-it-out-of-the-parking-lot beige, "gently used" but high mileage RAV4 and wandered down to the murky bayou. Weeping willows arched over the water and the breeze stirred the tapered, fingerlike leaves. I sat on a picnic table. Why had I come here? This was not a low-key thing. Oh, right. I think it was something about those lips and that lush, long body.

And if I didn't have the balls to be a bad boy, maybe I could have a secret meet with a bad girl?

She eased in beside me.

Where had she come from?

"So, Silent Sam. Here I am, I am."

Black tights, black bike shorts, black tank top. Black boots. Dark spiked hair. But her grin was goofy. I didn't expect goofy. Filled with a promise of fun. I grinned back without thinking. "What's this about?"

"About?" She danced her fingers in the air. "Does it have to be about something?"

"Have it your way," I said and turned back to the sluggish bayou. What was this bullshit?

Skye slid from the tabletop to the bench and snuggled her head onto my thigh. "Tough guy."

I didn't answer. I was seventeen and my bemoaned and as yet unrelieved virginity had made me unreliable in matters of character appraisal.

"I picked you out," she whispered.

"What?"

"I. Picked. You. Out." She said each word slow and separate, like she was speaking to someone more than slightly stupid.

"Picked me out? Why?"

She grinned up at me. Impish and certain of herself. "That's for me to know."

"You're crazy," I said.

She shrugged. "Old news."

She kidnapped my hand and pulled me down next to her. Sliding one hand behind my neck she gentled me forward and kissed me. Sweet and long. Her skull earring danced against my cheek.

I didn't know what she wanted and I didn't trust her. But that kiss. I wanted that.

▬

We sat in silence until she turned her moon-pale face up to the night.

"Do the stars weep?"

She looked at me, the heavy black line around her eyes smudged with new tears.

I had the urge to slide my arm from around her, careful, slow, before a trap closed on it. This was loony shit.

I took the coward's way instead. "Weep?" I snorted a laugh imitation. "What's a nineteenth-century word like that doing coming from a twenty-first-century, multi-pierced, multi-tattooed kind of girl?"

She brushed my arm away. "I think they weep. They weep for the people who can't."

This was piling up higher and deeper and I didn't, couldn't answer her.

"I have to go," she said. "Maybe you aren't the right one."

Skye was the poster girl for weird and so much not my type, but that hint of rejection punched my buttons.

"Maybe I am," I said. "Sure I am."

Skye

The next morning, Skye was waiting at my locker. Wearing black tights and a skirt made of duct tape. Lengths of tape each doubled back on itself and sewn to the piece alongside; the bottom was cut into fringe high on her fabulous thighs. The waistband was a man's tie. White lace top over a black lace bra. She was a neon sign screaming "SEX." I didn't mind licking the hollow of her throat in the park, but talking to her under the judgmental eye of the school population was not an option. I said nothing as I worked my combination lock.

Skye smiled and chuckled low and sex-smug next to my ear. "Oh, you're much cleverer than I thought. Great. You might be the one after all." She traced her finger down my cheek, a butterfly landing, and then touched it to her lips. "Mmmmmm." She tucked a note into my shirt pocket and she shimmered away.

I turned from my locker to see Taylor Banks staring at me.

This wasn't good. Not good at all.

Ken & Jeremy

At lunch, Skye sashayed past with the remains of a salad on her plate, and dropped a wadded napkin on my tray. Ken, with his Barbie name but unchiseled features, raised his eyebrows. I picked up my tray and took it to the dump window. I slid the napkin into my pocket.

"A note from Gothgirl?" Ken asked when I returned to the table.

"Didn't look," I said, way casual. "I assume she's just being annoying. The girl's brain is supposed to be slipping gears."

"Rumor one is she won't eat anything unless it's green. Rumor two is that she fucks anything with a pulse." This from Jeremy. Another piece of walking mist. Unlike Ken and me, Jeremy actually possessed a personality, but he kept it hidden in his locker during school hours. Lackluster was our trio's byword. Humiliation and head thumpings had taught us our place in the school's caste system during middle school.

"That lets us out on both counts," I said. "Library," I said. "Later."

I slid my see-through, school-approved mesh backpack over my shoulder and moved away from the tables. Around the first corner, I retrieved the napkin. An e-mail address: "Stormyskye@Email.net."

Not being a liar, I scooted to the library, grabbed a computer, and logged on. Working as guest, I got into my home account and pulled up a blank message and typed,

Mattman742@hotdrop.net.

I sent it to her address.

"I can do cryptic, too," I said to myself and hauled my cryptic butt to class.

Skye

I got home, shouted a hello to my little sister and what sounded like two dozen, but looked to be only three, of her friends, skipped my happy-hour Coke float, and bee-lined to the computer.

Her post was there. Lavender background, purple letters—

Same place. Midnight.

Midnight. I didn't bother to tell myself it wasn't going to happen. And I didn't bother to listen to my head muttering, why me, why me, whyme whymewhyme?

Katy

"What was the important e-mail?" Katy asked.

I got a Coke out of the fridge and sat on a barstool. "Huh?"

She pointed a big spoon at me. "You come in, ignore your Coke-and-ice-cream grossness, and hit the Net. What else could it be?"

Morgan, Reagan, and Sarah sat at the table, faces expectant.

Not only could Katy not share space with Skye, I wasn't telling anything to the big-mouth triplets.

"Do you have a girlfriend, Matt?" Morgan asked.

"I'm waiting for you to get to high school next year," I said.

They made rude blatting noises. "You, like, graduate this year. And besides, you're a . . ." Sarah didn't have a word for me. She flapped her hands. The others nodded, agreeing with—whatever.

"Do you ingrates ever expect me to drive you to the mall again? To the movies?"

Katy bonked Sarah on the head with the spoon. "Be nice to my brother," she said.

I nodded to her. "Thank you, Katy."

"You should always be kind to the hired help," she finished.

Humbled by middle schoolers, but off the hook about my e-mail, I left the room. And waited for midnight.

Skye

She was there first. Camos and a tummy-baring black tee. Stretched out on the table, looking like a star-kissed corpse. Spooky.

"There a reason you picked the witching hour?"

She didn't open her eyes. "Yes."

I waited. She waited longer.

"Okay, I'll play. Why midnight?"

"I had to see if you'd run with the big dogs." She stretched her arms over her head, languid and seemingly boneless. The tee rose higher, giving me a glimpse of round, braless breasts.

She sat up, swaying.

Whoa, I thought. Like she needs drugs to make her spacey.

"I was being tested?" I asked, knowing that I needed to leave. Walk. Away. Now.

Her slow-motion blink and lip lick set my beeper to vibrate.

"Mmmm, yep," she murmured. "You passed." Skye extended her hand palm up. "Come get your reward."

I pulled her to her feet. She slid into my arms, slinking and melding her body onto mine.

After a while, she pulled back. "Not all at once."

I pulled my shirttail out of my pants. Camouflage.

"What's the deal with you anyway?" Skye asked as she oozed back onto the bench.

"Me?"

"Yeah, you're like . . ." Pausing to think, she did the slow-mo lip thing again. "Umm . . . clear nail polish. People look right past it."

I shoved my hands in my pockets and stood hip-shot and—in my own mind—totally in charge. "I'm an under-the-radar kind of guy. If I can't be one of the golden ones, I'll stay the hell out of sight. Making yourself too visible plants a bull's-eye on your forehead."

Skye nodded. "True. I can't manage it, though." She made a low-flying motion with her hand.

"No kidding."

"But it's what's most important about you," Skye said. "That whole blend-into-the-background thing." She sat up as straight as she could manage. "I need to tell you about my mother and stepfather."

I snugged in next to her.

"But not now," she said and kissed me again.

I found a note on my bed when I sneaked into the house. "Late night ramble. I smell a girl."

Katy was too damn smart. And she had pushed her way into the wrong compartment.

Taylor

Skye avoided me at school and I returned the favor. But when we passed each other in the hall electricity arced between us. I was glad we didn't have classes together or my clothes would have spontaneously combusted.

That went on for two days. On the third day, Taylor Banks stood in front of my homeroom door.

"Matt, can I talk to you a sec?"

Being noticed didn't fit into my comfort zone. In days I had been seen by two who shouldn't have seen. I didn't know whether to be flattered or pissed, or concerned. That Taylor Banks was one of the chosen compounded the distress factor. Silvercool hair, eyes wide and dark, straight white teeth, curved tan body, and a soap opera name. Not the kind of girl who speaks to nobodies.

I nodded and she pointed toward the auditorium. I held the door open for her. When it sighed shut, it left us in shadow.

"Umm, I don't know how to say this and it's not really my business, but . . ."

She paused but I didn't help her out.

"It's about Skye," she said.

I still didn't help.

"Okay, it's, like, um, you need to be careful."

Nothing.

I could hear nerves in her voice, but this kind of girl had too much poise to pick at her nails or fiddle with her hair. "Oooo-kaaaay, I can see that you don't want to go the long way around. But, you need to know she's . . . dangerous if you get sucked in."

Taylor opened the door and the light slashed her face. "Call me if you want to know more. If not . . . then . . . well, take care of yourself."

Why didn't I want to admit to knowing Skye? What had kept me from running this by my friends or my sister? What could they tell me about Skye Colby?

She's the girl seen hanging around the cybercafés; always out at odd hours in marginal places. She smoked with greasy-haired, skinny guys sporting long-distance stares under the corner street lamps.

I had run into her once at WIRED. My printer crashed as I finished my research paper, and I made a panic-fueled three A.M. run to this least reputable but always open cybercafé. And there was Skye. Holding court with the java junkies and chat room addicts.

The testosterone-fueled jocks called her slut puppy, the bland blondes in the plaid skirts wrinkled their snub noses in distaste, the teachers called her brilliant, and the counselors called her unstable.

She was all that. And I'd get attention I'd worked hard to avoid if I were seen with her. And her reputation embarrassed me. But if I played it right, soon she was going to take me to paradise. Taylor Banks wasn't going to. Ever.

Ken & Jeremy

I hooked up with Ken, pizza, and beer in front of Jeremy's big-screen TV. Popping the first one, Ken handed it to me. "Did you hear that Gothgirl got kicked to the bricks?"

I worked hard at expressionless. "Nope."

"Jeremy was there."

Jeremy nodded enthusiastically, his mouth full of double cheese and pepperoni. He chewed and swallowed as he made those wait-a-minute-I'm-eating hand gestures. Like we couldn't process that fact ourselves.

"She's in my English class. We're reading *The Crucible*. Fisk trying to get a discussion going, asks if there's a contemporary group that judges and condemns before there's proof of guilt." He swigged his beer. More hand flapping. "And because we're all stupid and apathetic she's waving a newspaper in front of us."

Jeremy laughed. "So anyway, Skye says, 'Sororities and cheerleaders.'"

Ken snorted. "That's too cool."

"And," Jeremy continued, "Ann Fields is sitting right there."

Ann Fields. Head cheerleader and Tri Delt triple legacy.

"So Ann says, 'Bitch!'"

"I so wish I could've been there," Ken said.

"Skye, quick as a snake, fired her textbook at Ann. Bam, right in the mouth. Major bloodletting. Lots of screaming."

I reached for pizza, keeping my head down and facial expression out of sight.

"Fisk asks, 'Why'd you throw that book?' And Skye" —Jeremy grinned—"Skye says, like it should be evident to a toad, 'I didn't have a stone handy.'"

And I half remembered something. Taylor called Skye dangerous. Ann called her a bitch and got clocked in the face. There. I had it. Skye. Ninth grade. Not yet Goth. Suddenly changed from awkward to awesome. Dark, mysterious, and sexily beautiful. A Senior Football Stud made his move. And then the rumor. That stupid rumor that goes around every high school. "She did the whole team right on the field." I doubt anyone even believes it, but the girl gets branded the school slut anyway. But in Skye's case, the morning after Homecoming, the starting line awoke to find their cars had broken windshields. Every last one.

Skye turned Goth. People turned away. But they didn't call her names. Not to her face. I guess Ann forgot.

I sighed. Skye fascinated me. But high school is not a place for courting the hatred of the upper crust or hanging with those who do. People like me didn't want to know people like Skye. I made up my mind not to see her again. Paradise postponed. Hell, cancelled. My adolescence officially sucked out loud.

Katy

Katy was waiting in the kitchen with my Coke float in front of her. "Drink up and tell me about the girl."

I took the Coke and swigged. "What girl?"

She grabbed the glass and poured the contents down the sink. "Loss of privileges," she said. "You have a girlfriend and I want details."

I was suddenly ashamed. I thought about it from the other side. I had been planning on having sex with a girl I didn't even like, would never admit to knowing. How sleazy was that? Did I want Katy to ever behave that way? Worse—what would I think of a guy who would treat her the way I had planned on treating Skye?

I didn't know Skye's motives for choosing me. But I knew mine. I was an asshole. That almost qualified me for popularity.

"Is there kissing?" Katy asked. "I want to hear about the kissing. Is there other stuff? I have to hear about the other stuff."

I told Katy the absolute truth. "I don't have a girlfriend."

"Liar," Katy said.

—

I hadn't lied to Katy about a girlfriend, but I was a liar. I had been lying to Katy since I was ten years old. My parents had been lying to her for longer than that.

Even if I didn't have a sitcom cutesy-close family, there was a built-in belief system. I mean, my parents weren't falling-down drunks and didn't beat the crap out of me as a pastime, so I trusted them. Until I was ten. If Katy knew what I knew—she wouldn't have trust, either.

Because when I was ten and Katy was six, a man came to our house.

Matt

A man came to our house. It was summer and I answered the door.

He said, "You must be Matt."

I remember, even now, the feeling that something was wrong. He looked like a nice man, but the air around him was wrong. Mom walked up and she didn't smile or say hello. And the wrong feeling got worse. Mom didn't introduce me. She took me aside and said that she had put Katy down with a video and would I do her a big favor and go to my room. And please shut my door. She stood there until I went upstairs.

I waited until I heard them go into the den; then I went to the top of the stairs and listened. Their conversation was long, most of it hushed and whispered. Sometimes Mom's voice would rise, then the man's would get a bit loud, and they would both quiet down again. I heard Katy's name several times. Finally, he left.

At dinner, Mom and Dad didn't talk. After Katy was asleep and I was sent to bed, Mom and Dad started to argue.

I heard that loud and clear.

When you're a little kid, you never think about your parents and whether they are in love. But I found out then that not all parents are. In love. The argument I heard must have been a rehash of an old one. My mother told my dad that he forced her into the affair. That he paid her no attention and—I don't remember all of it.

It hurt me to hear it. It hurts now.

My father yelled that he had done everything for her, for us. Instead of leaving her, he had put up the money for Mom's business so she wouldn't be working for that lowlife lawyer anymore. And he'd accepted Katy as his own. She couldn't ask him to do this. He wouldn't.

Things got a little blurry then. I was a kid, but I knew what he meant. Dad wasn't Katy's father.

I felt as if someone had scooped my insides out like a Halloween pumpkin.

How was I was supposed to feel, to think about Mom? Dad?

Katy?

I listened more. If everything I had believed in was gone, I had to know what to believe now.

The pieces I could put together were that Mom had an affair with a married lawyer, and Katy was not my sister, but my half sister.

My half sister. How do you have half a sister?

Mr. Lawyer didn't want his wife to know. He had kids.

Are those kids more his than Katy? Is Katy a half child?

My dad didn't divorce my mom, and his name is on Katy's birth certificate. Mr. Lawyer agreed to this and said he'd never try to contact Katy or Mom again.

I guess Katy was less than a half child.

How much of a child was she to Dad?

But Mr. Lawyer's wife dumped him and moved away with their children. Mr. Lawyer has decided that Katy is his child now. He showed up at our house, asking to visit Katy. He wanted to tell her that he's Daddy.

Mom thought it was okay for Sleazebag to visit, but not to spew the truth. Dad went into emotional orbit.

I guess in the final shakeout, Mom told the guy to get lost, because I never saw him again. But I'm always watching over my shoulder, waiting for him to show up again.

So for the last seven years, I had info I didn't want, didn't need, and didn't know what to do with.

Before, my parents were mostly absent, but I could count on them. I suppose I still could, but there was a big rip in my safety net. If I didn't tell Katy what I knew, then wasn't I lying to her every day of my life? But why make her feel as confused as I did?

And the weird thing is, it made me feel more protective than ever of Katy. If she had no real dad and only half a brother, then I had to love her twice as hard.

And I learned not to like surprises. And that's when I started building boxes, compartments, and files. Mom and Dad had two each. Mom had one box for the betrayer of our family, and another as the mom I loved. Dad had his father box and the box I kicked him into when he went weird around Katy. If he wanted to be weird around Mom, that's one thing, but Katy didn't do shit to him.

I'd always been a shy kid, but now I expected the worst of people. I hit the big sifter called middle school at the same time I learned about misplaced trust. A double whammy. So, I built my box, too. I liked it. And I did my ghost-of-the-corridors thing. Ghosts do not have relationships, and that seemed like a good plan to me.

But I'd gone into the box when I was little and it was getting claustrophobic. I wanted to be out of it now, but was too afraid to leave.

Maybe I was looking for someone to show me how to break out.

Skye

In our school, the transgressor is not so much kicked out of classes as kicked into alternative school to serve suspension days. Insult is added by requiring that the transgressor's parents keep their moppet under house arrest during nonschool hours.

Skye's parents must have taken it to heart. I didn't even get e-mail. That was a relief. As long as I was dumping her, it was easier to do it with her cooperation.

The three days were uneventful. Back to my fade-into-the-paint status. But while I was crawling the Web at home, an IM binged its way onto my screen.

Ditch school tomorrow. Meet me at my house.

Lust and interest resurfaced.

Sanity won. I took a deep breath and logged off.

Skye wasn't at school the next day. Friday. She showed up Monday wearing leather pants and a T-shirt that proclaimed, "REHAB IS FOR QUITTERS." She was kicked right back into alternative school for skipping. Rumor was five days this go 'round.

Katy

"Misty has decided to be anorexic," Katy said.

We were munching popcorn in front of the TV. Katy was indulging me by participating in my favorite pastime. Reruns. When I'm not in school or studying, I'm in front of the television. Must have caught the bug from the former baby-sitter. But I only watch cable reruns. The chance to become involved or to be surprised existed if I watched something in real time. I don't like either feeling. So I tune into series that are a couple of years old.

"Decided? I thought it was like a disease."

Katy crunched her popcorn and swallowed while she shook her head. "Misty says it's not a disease, it's a lifestyle choice." She said the last part like she was quoting an idiot.

Misty was one of Katy's one hundred best friends and she was already thin, as well as ready to bloom into beautiful. She would be one of the goldens for sure. Katy would, too.

"And what do you think?" I asked.

Katy chomped a bit more. That alone told me she wasn't planning on starvation as a lifestyle choice.

“I think her mind is as skinny as her butt.”

I love Katy. She takes no prisoners.

Skye

But Skye took me prisoner.

By the time she got back to classes, I hadn't seen Skye for two weeks. I thought I had worked my way out of thrummin' and strummin' for the girl. After school, I was cramming books in my pack and she appeared next to me. She breathed in my ear. "This is a little present for you."

She pulled her face around so I could see her and slid her tongue out. A round gold stud glinted there.

"E me if you're interested." And she was gone.

And so was I.

My post to her contained only the word—"When?" I was back in cryptic mode, telling myself I was in control of the situation.

My house. Saturday. 1:00.

I guessed that only Skye would be home. Okay, I prayed no one else would be there and my chance at a divine experience was finally at hand.

I arrived at her lower-end middle-class neighborhood. House and yard neat and carefully kept. Ordinary. I guess I thought Skye would live in something Gothic and overgrown. I knocked on the door.

From inside, Skye yelled, "I got it," and popped the door open. "In," she commanded. "Follow my lead."

A little girl, maybe five years old, sat in front of the television. She sucked her thumb. "Lisa, this is Bob Wilson. Can you say hello?"

Bob Wilson?

The child looked up and pulled her thumb from her mouth. Her lip hung slack and her eyes told me her story. Down's syndrome.

"Hey, Lisa," I said. Lisa opened and closed her fingers in a kind of crabbed wave and replaced her thumb as she turned back to the cartoons.

"I'm gone," Skye yelled toward the kitchen as she pushed me out the front door. I was already on the porch when I heard her mother.

"Skye, come back in here."

She put her hand to my chest, stopping me from returning inside, then stuck her head around the doorframe. "What?" she demanded.

"What's going on?"

Skye sighed. "I told you, Bob and I are going to the library and he's gonna help me with my make-up work."

"The tutor the counselor set you up with?"

"Right. I'll be back for supper."

Skye slammed the door and pushed me off the porch. "Let's get the hell out of Dodge."

Once in the car, she said, "Beach." I drove.

▬

"I think we need to talk," I said.

"Sure," she grinned and winked at me. "Bob."

"We can start there."

She crossed her legs yoga-style. I watched the road, rather than her face, but I swear I could hear her roll her eyes. "My parents are toxic. I like you and I don't want them to know who you are. Don't even want them to see you. They'll ruin it."

Little inconsistency? "Why did you have me come to your house then?"

Skye jutted her chin out and nibbled her lower lip. "I wanted you to see Lisa. She's part of the situation." She shook her shoulders like a dog shedding rain. "We'll talk about that later."

A white cat darted across the street and I slowed.

"Speed up and hit it," Skye said, her voice urgent.

"Hit it?"

Sighing, she leaned back against the seat. "Too late." She cricked her neck back and forth, then rubbed the nape with her fingers. "I hate white animals."

In a nanosecond, I had become Bob the tutor, was introduced into some as yet undetermined conspiracy connected to Skye's sister, and had been instructed to go assassin on animals of the pale kind. Strange had taken on a whole new level of complexity.

Skye noticed my bafflement. She shrugged. "I just don't like them, you know."

"So they ought to die?"

She nodded, careless and unconcerned. "They're in my way."

My laugh was nervous. Not good for a man pretending to be cool. "Meaning, they shouldn't live in your world?"

"Now you're catching on." Case closed. She looked at me. "Why do you ignore me at school?"

I blushed. "Okay, I'm an asshole, but . . . Skye . . ."

"Hmmm," she hummed, deep in her throat. She held her index finger up and tapped it toward me. "You think I make a habit of playing in traffic and you don't want to join me there, right?"

Startled by her finding the words for my scrambled thoughts, I blushed again.

"Geez, Matt, I'm weird, not stupid. You're like, ex—cu—sed. I like it that way."

"Why?" I asked, taking the feeder onto the interstate to Galveston.

"School is the same thing as my parents. If we go public, we'll become something 'they' poison with their comments."

The girl the school decreed morally bankrupt wanted to keep our relationship hidden because she liked me. Wanted to protect me. And me, Mr. He's-Fine-I-Guess-I-Never-Hear-Anything-Bad-About-Him wanted to keep the relationship a secret so I could bang the school's crazy slut and not be ridiculed for it.

I kept driving.

I parked close to Sixty-first Street and we walked along the seawall. The waves were kicking up, the wind fierce and a little too cool for comfort, so there were few people out. We huddled close together on a bench.

"We've got a little prob," Skye said. She opened her mouth. Around the welcome-to-the-world-of-wonder stud was red, puffy tongue.

"That looks painful," I said.

"That would be the prob," Skye said and snuggled her head against my neck.

I sighed. Okay, I would try not to be a complete shit. "You wanted me to see your sister. Tell me about it. Her, I mean."

Skye shifted a little so that the back of her head rested against my shoulder. "You need a quick trip to Skye's past to understand it all. Ready for a journey to the dark forest?"

I nodded.

"There's one thing you have to promise."

"Sure," I said, thinking I wasn't so sure.

"No pity. I don't feel sorry for myself and I hate it if anyone else does."

I grinned in a way that I hoped was charming. "I only feel pity for myself; that takes up all my time."

"Good." She settled back. "First, my mother got pregnant when she was not quite fourteen. By a married man. Second, she was too stupid to get the pic and by the time she figured out that her stomach was filled with more than gas . . ."

"Too late for an abortion," I said.

"Yup, and third, her snake-handler, religious-zealot parents deposited her on the curb."

"Nice," I said. And my self-pity switched over to Skye. Just a little.

Skye flipped one hand as if chasing something away. "She trolled the streets, doing I-don't-want-to-know-what, and when I entered the world, I was shipped off to foster care."

She paused and I looked down into her face. Blank. She watched the waves as if she were measuring them.

"I don't know how many places I was in as a baby," Skye said. "And Mom says there's no way I can remember this, but I do, I swear." She sat up and locked her stare onto me. "I remember screaming my lungs out in a crib and nobody coming. Just screaming and crying and sobbing and . . . nothing . . . nobody."

The waves were crashing harder now and spray misted around us.

Skye pulled in a deep breath, turning her face back out to the waves. "It seems Mom had a prob with coke. She was in and out of rehab as often as I changed foster homes. Every so often, she'd clean up, get a real job, and take me back. Never lasted long, and boom, I was back in the system."

Skye stood abruptly. "Let's walk."

She reached into her pocket and pulled out a small digital camera.

"This was a revolving-door kind of thing until I was

about twelve. Mom straightened up and was working in a coffeehouse. She met Lex."

Skye's voice had been even, almost monotonous as she told her story, like she was reading a phone book. But she said "Lex" as if her tongue throbbed.

We walked in silence, and she snapped pics of the few fools on the beach in this wind. An old man surf fishing, a speed walker, a mother admonishing her children. She photographed in stealth mode, and no one appeared to be aware of her camera. We started back for the bench.

"So." Skye slipped the camera back into her pocket. "Lex. He was nondrug, had a legal job and all his teeth. Mom was in luuuuuv."

"What's he do?"

"Hmmm, he works for his brother's company. They fix house foundations. And he does this thing where he buys broken-down houses, fixes them up, and resells them."

"Sounds pretty good."

"To my mom, it was great. They got married, pulled me out of foster care, and moved me here."

I slid my arm from around her and picked up her hand. I lifted it to my lips, looked Skye straight in the eyes, and kissed her palm, then folded her fingers over the kiss.

She stared at her hand. Her blank expression didn't change. But she nodded. I didn't know what that meant.

"We need to get home," she said, as she pulled her hand from mine and strode away.

We didn't talk on the way home. Skye curled up on the seat, her head resting on my thigh, and went to sleep.

I hadn't been feeling much about Skye except lust and confusion, but maybe now guilt was working at me. Maybe if nobody else would love her, I needed to. I was overwhelmed with—I don't know—the white knight syndrome. I wanted to help, to protect this girl. Maybe sex would happen between us. Sure, I hoped it would, but it was different now. I would never be like the others, using her for sex and then tossing her away. I had found the real Skye. I'd save her.

She had picked me out.

Skye

Monday, I was still in my armor and riding my white horse as I waited by Skye's locker with a rose in my hand. She entered the hall and freeze-framed. When she recovered she turned her back to my rose, her locker, and me, and walked away. The brief second we made eye contact, her stare was lethal.

—

I tossed the rose in the trash and wandered off, pulling at my eyelashes, something I do when I'm major whacked. Hell, what had I done? I showed the little kid screaming in the crib that someone would be there for her.

At home, the door wasn't finished slamming behind me when I logged onto my e-mail server and found her post:

8. Park.

Katy

Katy rapped twice on my door, then barged in. Her usual habit. She carried one of those magazines for teen girls.

"Do you think I'm a Gamma girl?"

"And a Gamma girl would be . . .?"

"You need to tune into the news, read the newspaper, something beside watch reruns and have secret meetings with a secret girl. Is she real ugly or what?"

Katy was going to grow up to be a lawyer or a cop. If I didn't strangle her first.

She reminded me of Skye a little that way.

I blinked, then chased that thought right out of my head before it could do damage.

"What's a Gamma girl?" I asked.

She perched on my bed. "See, there's Alpha girls, they are A-list, always dressed just so, hair the latest cut, cheerleaders, popular. They can be nice, but mostly they're bitchy."

Ann Fields, I thought, for the bitchy anyway. Taylor Banks might be a nice Alpha.

"Hold it," I said. I pulled up my favorite computer program, the one with every kind of graph or chart known to mankind, and marked some percentile points.

"So, am I an Alpha?"

"Nope. Clothes and hair alone kick you out of Alpha." I pointed to the graph. "You're practically flat-lined. The bitchy part might be right."

Katy dressed for comfort. She was a fab soccer player and wore her long hair pulled back in a ponytail most of the time.

"Okay, I'm ignoring the bitchy part. But I might decide to remember it later." She shot me her mean look. "Then there's the Beta girl." Katy read from the magazine. "For B list. Will do almost anything to be a friend of an Alpha. Constantly diets, ever aspiring for popularity."

I tapped more arbitrary point awards. "Nope, you're not a Beta. You eat Betas for breakfast."

Katy grinned. "Cool."

She read again. "Gamma girls. Not an A-lister, but doesn't care. Good grades, into sports, aspires to a good university. Has friends. Comfortable in her own skin. Independent and can be slightly quirky."

"And we have a winner," I said. I pointed to the steadily peaking line. "You're a Gamma."

"I didn't finish." She read, "Usually church-oriented and has close relationship with parents."

"Oops," I said. I placed a point at the bottom of the scale. "Can you be a Gamma minus?"

Katy sighed. "Yeah. I don't think the church and parents would be a deal breaker. But if you read the whole article, it says that the reason a Gamma is so comfortable and confident is the closeness and support of her parents."

Mom was always working and Dad was, well, the ghost of our house. He was distant with me, but just plain odd with Katy. When Katy was popping with enthusiasm, her usual state, Dad seemed to draw into himself and leave the room. Before that summer afternoon seven years ago, I thought it was strange.

"You know, Matt," Katy interrupted my thoughts. "I do have the closeness and support of my parents—if you can be considered my parents. I mean, you've raised me more than Mom and Dad."

Katy rolled up the magazine and thwacked me on the head with it and sailed from the room. Unconcerned and totally at ease with what she had just said. Yep, Gamma girl. I changed the point to the top of the graph. All the way.

Skye

Later, I told Katy I was going to Ken's to study, and got to the park early. I sat on the picnic table, considering my sin, and again Skye materialized beside me.

She didn't seem angry. "Stand up," she said. Atonal. No clues. I stood, and she swung from the shoulder, landing a full-on punch to my left jaw. I staggered and cursed as lights danced behind my eyelids.

"You could have ruined everything," she said. Still not visibly angry, her voice was low and determined. "You will never pull a move like that again."

"I don't—"

"That's right. You don't. No one, but no one is to know about us. Got that?" She whirled away from me, then spun and came back. "Have you told anyone about me? Does anyone know?"

Taylor Banks flashed through my head, but I wasn't about to admit anything. I hadn't said a word to Taylor, so it wasn't quite a lie.

"I didn't know you were serious about this other-people-will-poison-it thing," I said, massaging my jaw. "Damn, Skye, that hurt."

When I looked up, she was running through the trees, vanishing into her dark forest.

I should have known better.

I needed time to process this multiple personality thing Skye was working. I wouldn't get angry or even hurt. I would ride the mellow and wait to see what she did next.

Ken & Jeremy

When I got home, Katy was hanging up the phone. "That was Jeremy."

I thanked the god that looks after lying little shits that Jeremy had called and not Ken.

"His brother, Brad, wants to take both of you to a frat party and show you around campus next weekend."

While neither Jeremy nor I had high caliber GPAs, we did have substantially hefty SAT scores. We were already accepted to the University of Texas, where Brad was a Phi Delt. "Sweet," I said.

Skye

I went to school, came home, and went to school again. While I was there, I ignored Skye, but I paid enough attention to know that she was in and out of the counselor's office more than she was in the halls or class. Ann Fields's parents filed suit against Skye for assaulting their dear one. A compromise was reached, and Skye had to have anger management sessions with the school shrink.

I found myself missing her when I heard that session one ended with Skye inviting the shrink to perform a sexual act upon his person that was physically impossible for all but the most adept contortionist. Session two ended when she wadded the handouts he gave her and set them on fire in his wastebasket.

Ann Fields showed her less-than-perky nature when she spray-painted "SKYE IS A SLUTE" on Skye's locker. It was anyone's guess as to whether the final e was a reference to Skye's name or evidence of the airhead-cheerleader cliché.

A dead rat—a ripely, seriously dead rat—appeared in Ann's locker soon thereafter. Most of the riff and the raff were amused, but I worried that Skye was coming unspooled. And, hell, where'd she get a rat? And I wondered if it was white.

Katy

"Can my big brother take his little sis to the bookstore?"

"Sure, but why do you need a book fix?"

Katy had adopted my habit of reading mostly classics. I read and reread things like *The Arabian Nights*, *The Man in the Iron Mask*, and anything with King Arthur. If I couldn't be a hero, I wanted to read about them. Katy did *The Secret Garden* and stuff with plucky girl characters.

She grabbed the Visa from the desk drawer. Mom allows us to use it as long as we keep the charges in bounds and for sane-person purchases like books, school supplies, and haircuts.

In the car, Katy rummaged in my glove box until she found my candy stash.

"Does that come under vegetarian?" I asked.

"Nothing in these but sugar. Never mooed, never had a face." Her forehead creased. "Now, I think refined sugar is pretty much poison, but it's not an animal product. So it gets a little hazy." She popped the SweetTarts back into the box. Sighed. "That's why I need a vegetarian cookbook."

She turned toward me with her patented Katy goofy-grin/wicked-laugh combo. "The vegetarian cookbook most recommended has 'moose' in the title." Another wicked laugh. "I love contradictions."

Since at this point I was a living contradiction, I wasn't as enthusiastic.

"I want something on Buddhism, too."

I shot her the Big-Brother-Looks-Askance arched eyebrow thing.

"One of those Buddhism for the Brain Dead kind of books. See if I'm the Zen type."

"Katy. Can I remind you that while other children, me being one of them, are always, but always scared shitless in *The Wizard of Oz* when those damned winged monkeys showed up, you loved them?"

"Yeah," she said. "They were so cool. Remember, you got so sick of me wanting to see that part that you made cardboard wings and superglued them to Curious George's back?"

"This is my point. There is no Zen in evil-monkey liking. If you're feeling Zen, you must be about to go into a coma."

Katy proved my point by flipping me a very non-Zen middle finger.

She got the books and skimmed through them on the way home. "Did you know that mashed-up chickpeas are called hummus?"

Back at home, I hit the Net, checked out MSN's most-searched sites list, and cruised a couple of those. An IM pinged on.

Tonight. Park.

Skye

She was waiting when I drove up. Cutoff shorts, halter top, combat boots. Big metal cross on a heavy chain. "I'm taking you somewhere," she said as she popped into the car. "Drive to the Woodlands."

The Woodlands was a high-end community on the north side of Houston, more than an hour away.

Without a word, I pulled out of the park and headed north.

"Good boy, you're learning."

"As long as you don't hit me again," I said. "What's up?"

"It's a surprise."

I flinched. "I'm not big on surprises."

"Do you want to play it safe all your life?"

Her voice was soft, but intent. It was an inquiry, not a complaint.

"Good question. I guess I don't know."

She settled her head back and smiled gently. "Then let me be the unpredictable one and you just drive where I point. You can be blameless and I can be good for something."

Soft thunder rolled ominously, and a faraway bolt of

lightning flashed. Skye warned me that I could tell no one of this trip.

"You're not one of those guys that keep a journal are you?"

I hesitated, wondering.

"Oh, you are, aren't you? Do you keep it on your computer or in a book?" Skye had done a zero to sixty on the agitation meter in about three seconds.

"Whoa. Not guilty," I said.

"You're lying."

I grabbed the wheel like I was strangling it. "I'm not lying. I don't keep a journal. I'm too boring to keep a journal."

That seemed to disconnect her current. "I guess that's true."

Thanks.

"Why the big hesitation when I asked?" she said.

"It's a weird question. Why would you want to know that?"

She settled back into the seat. "I've got reasons."

I let it go.

She bitched about Lex installing a security system, hoping to keep her from doing her Houdini act at night.

"So, how'd you get out?"

"Window," she said.

"He's not dumb enough not to have armed the windows, is he?"

"Nope, they're wired. But a magnet on the contact—and poof, you're gone and no alarm."

I was amazed. Okay, and amused and even envious.

This girl could wear all black all the time and still be rainbow colorful. Con artists. You gotta love 'em.

When we reached the Woodlands, Skye directed me to what looked like a music store/head shop combo.

We parked and went in. Pink flyers roamed the door and the counter. "IT'S ROLLIN'!" they announced. Nothing else was on the paper but today's date. Skye picked one up. "Where?" she asked the guy behind the counter. He was reading a comic book.

"Humble. Look for a private airfield. About twenty minutes out. It's not a comm. But there's laser, so the cops could show."

Skye nodded like this made sense. "Thanks." She motioned me out.

We got in the car. "You know how to get to Humble?"

"Sure, but what was all that?"

"Want to go to a rave?"

I thought a minute. It was a bad-boy thing to do. Matt Lathrop. A rave. And on a school night.

I started the car and headed for the interstate.

"Can you translate what that guy said?"

"Okay, you do know what a rave is, right? You're not that backward?"

I sighed and shot her a replica of the Katy look. "Yes, I know what a rave is. Gimme a break."

"All righty then." She was grinning and goofy now. I grinned back. Infected.

"That was what's called a 'map point.'"

"Map point?"

"Right, the place advertises the rave."

"It did?"

"Sure, the pink paper, 'rollin',' and the date. That tells you it's a rave and when. Go there that day, ask where, and the guy tells you."

"What's 'rollin''?"

She shook her head. "You're such a virgin."

She didn't know how right she was.

"When you take X, the ground feels like it rolls under you. There's always X at a rave."

I wasn't grinning anymore.

Skye noticed. "Don't worry. Neither of us is gonna roll tonight."

Okay, better.

"So, what was all the other stuff he said?"

"Hmm, it's not comm. Not a commercial rave. Raves have gotten kind of mainstream and big organizers do some of them. This is a smaller, more 'in the know' thing."

Now I really grinned. I was "in the know."

"There will be laser lights, which means probably trance music. The commercial raves are supposedly X-free and have cops around. Blind rent-a-cops mostly. But since laser lights can be seen, some local cops might come around—that's why we won't be rollin' tonight." She pointed. "Turn there."

I turned, we followed the off-ramp to a road that was little more than a path, and drove up to a field full of people. Light beams stabbed the sky.

Cars parked in a wide half circle, many with the headlights on. A band was on a stack of wooden pallets and what appeared to be a hastily constructed tarp/tent arrangement covered most of the instruments and a generator. The middle of the circle was a mass that seemed to move like a pot full of worms. A seething, gyrating mass that beat like a big heart to music and the lights. The thunder, louder now, closer, seemed to keep time.

Skye and I worked our way through the cars.

The music had her wired and fired. She goofed on me again, but her words were serious. "Do not stay on me like a fungus, until I look the crowd over. I want to see if I know anyone." She paused. "I know the drug guys, but it's not like they'll ever admit seeing us here."

"I don't . . ."

"Arrgggghhh!" she yelled, clutching handfuls of her hair as if to yank them out.

I held my hands up. "I surrender."

She gave me a loud, smacking kiss. "Thank you so much. Please, do not take anything anyone offers you. Not even water in a bottle. If someone walks up and says, 'E?' or 'X?' walk away. But smile." She raked her eyes over me, assessing. "God, you look so narc."

We reached the edge of the crowd. "Keep to the edges, watch, dance, have a good time. I'll be back."

And she was gone. That disappearing thing she had working was getting spooky.

Up close, I could make out individual bodies and most of the expressions were amazing. Like faces at a tent revival lost in religious rapture. My pulse pounded in time to the beat, and the flash of lights—pink, blue, green, yellow, white—made the dancers appear and disappear, close and far, and then back close. My body moved in time, hypnotized.

There was a cool breeze, but the dancers, wearing minimal clothes, were sweating. Tank tops, tube tops, bikini tops—exposed flesh, slick and shiny, heated my blood. Some of the ravers wore costumes—princesses, cartoon characters, space men, warlocks, and a few vampires. Guys moved through the crowd selling glow sticks, bracelets, and necklaces. The dancers waved the sticks, and the bracelets and necklaces gleamed against the dark as the dancers moved. My hypnosis escalated as I watched the neonlike light surge and ebb. And there were exposed belly buttons with flashing red lights, blinking lights pinned to clothing or set into headbands. Shoes with blinking lights set into the soles.

I watched, smiling, I think, spaced and definitely tranced, when someone bumped my shoulder. A huge man, shaggy-haired and very much not-tranced, leaned into my ear. "E?" The back of his knuckles brushed mine.

Before I could shake the spell of the music and lights, Skye appeared in front of him.

"He's not rollin' tonight, Squirrel." The man grinned and I saw the protruding front teeth that accounted for the name.

Squirrel shrugged and eeled away through the crowd.

"Come dance," Skye commanded.

She led me deep into the mass, then turned and

pushed close up against me. Her body undulated against mine, matching the throb of the music. She shimmied down, then back up, tracing a path of heat. I pushed back against her, trying for more contact, matching her moves. Her eyelids looked heavy and she never took her dark gaze from mine. I had never felt this alive. Everything pulsed and pounded and breathed deep.

Her eyes left mine, and then suddenly, she stopped, her attention diverted. She watched for a few seconds, almost vibrating. She strode away, pushing people aside. I saw Squirrel's head just above the crowd. Skye headed his way. I followed and finally saw what she had seen.

She reached Squirrel just as he was making the handoff, and slapped out. Something flipped onto the ground.

"What's your problem, bitch?" Squirrel wasn't grinning now.

Three girls, at most fourteen years old, stood there. Together they couldn't have weighed over two hundred pounds.

Skye ignored Squirrel and turned to the girls. "How much do you weigh?" she asked the skinniest one. "Seventy-five. Maybe eighty pounds?"

The girl, frightened, backed away. "Are you a cop?"

"That tab would roll a linebacker. What do you think it would do to you?"

All three girls were looking for a way out.

"Heart attack would be your best bet. Stroke. Whatever." She eyed the girls again. "God, you're already on downers, aren't you?"

She wheeled on Squirrel, who was on his knees, searching the trampled grass for his product. "Don't let me see you pushing to babies again, Squirrel."

"Get stuffed," Squirrel muttered.

Skye kicked him square in the forehead. "You know better than to fuck with me."

One of the girls wore a pacifier hung by a ribbon around her neck. Skye grabbed it and jerked, breaking the ribbon, then sailed the pacifier away in a lofty arc. "Go home, and on the way, have a Happy Meal and a milkshake and stop being so stupid."

She flared away, grabbing my arm as she passed, tugging me in her wake.

I wanted to be a hero, but right now, Skye was one. She was warrior-fierce and she was fabulous.

She pulled me around to face her, latched her eyes back onto mine, and moved against me in time to the music again. "Don't," she said when I opened my mouth. "I don't even want to talk about it."

The thunder cracked hard enough now to split the clouds and the rain sluiced down. The band scrambled to get the instruments under cover; the laser lights shut down. People ran for the safety of their cars. The field emptied out but a few danced on, so tranced that, for them, the music still played.

Skye stepped back from me and lifted her face to the rain. She stretched out her arms and the water streamed down them, coating her with a sheen. The lightning flashed and the car lights caught the shine, turning Skye into a gleaming—thing.

And she danced. Not the gyrating, sex-fueled dance of before, but she rose on her toes with her arms arched gracefully over her head. I had seen this before. When Katy had taken ballet. Then Skye moved to the side, stretching out one foot to a point, then moving the weight to her pointed toe and closing. It was slow, controlled, and her arms flowed with the movement of her legs. She continued to dance, spinning on one leg and then another like the ballerinas on music boxes, jumping—little feet-flicking jumps or great leaping jumps like a deer over a hedge. She did other moves, too, some of them not as practiced, but she was good. She wasn't great, but this was something that spoke of more than a few lessons.

Who was this girl? How did ballet fit with her tale of misery and abuse? The sight of her, the lightning making her glow, then darken, the rain making her flicker in the headlights—her beauty and her mystery overwhelmed me.

On the way home, I asked, "How long did you take ballet?"

"Didn't."

"My little sister took ballet when she was, like, seven or eight."

Skye watched the night slide past her window.

I decided on an indirect route, since Skye wasn't answering questions. "She was hilarious. Katy. My little sister."

No answer.

"She would wear the leotard and the tights and then put her soccer shorts on over the whole thing instead of the little flippy skirt."

Skye was still staring out the window, but I could tell she was listening.

"The ballet instructor lady—what do you call them?"

No response.

"Anyway," I continued. "The ballet instructor told Mom that Katy was an individualist and her creativity should be encouraged. So Katy kept wearing her soccer shorts."

I stopped. On cop shows, the detective stops and the guy being interrogated always fills the silence.

Skye watched the window a little more, then turned to me. "So, is there a point to this story of family harmony?"

"Huh?" I said. "Oh, not really. Just that when the recital came, or whatever you call that . . ." I stopped again. Nope, she wasn't falling for it. "Mom handed Katy her tutu. Katy looked at it like it was made of snail snot and said she wasn't wearing it. She put her soccer shorts on and we all went to the recital."

I stopped again.

Skye sighed. "Will you finish?"

"I guess that individuality only counted if there wasn't an audience, because the teacher told Katy that if she didn't wear the tutu, she couldn't dance in the recital."

"What did she do? Katy, I mean."

"She threw the tutu in the trash can right in front of the teacher and said 'It's your school. You can make the rules.' Then she grabbed my hand and said, 'Let's go home and watch *The Wizard of Oz.*'"

I smiled thinking about it. That might have been the night I put the wings on Curious George.

"And your parents let her leave?"

"Sure," I said. "Why wouldn't they?"

Skye shook her head like she couldn't believe what I'd said. "Amazing."

She settled back into her seat. "You really love Katy."

She said it like she was filing data.

"Yes. Like you love Lisa."

"Right," she said. "Like Lisa."

Wanna-be Frat Guy

Jeremy invited Ken to the frat party, but he announced that he had opened a new business.

Ken, of the ten-word vocabulary, an entrepreneur?

"I power-level," he told us.

Jeremy and I looked at each other, then resorted to Kenspeak. "Huh?"

Ken filled his not-school hours with a computer game. We called it Crack because Ken was a junkie for the thing. He played online with other geekoids. He played as a character and the character had levels of power. That much I knew.

"I put an ad on e-Bay," Jeremy said. "I'll play the game for another person's character and bring them up to the level they want. Ten bucks a level for the first forty, then twenty bucks a level from forty to sixty. We negotiate for the next twenty levels."

Jeremy and I were still stuck in the "huh?" category.

Ken rubbed his head, frustrated with our stupidity.

"Your character has no power at the beginning, and when you play online, somebody always kills you. That's not much fun. You keep having to start over."

We nodded, pretending this was rational.

"I've got my character up to the level one hundred and twenty. Loup-garou is pretty invincible."

"Werewolf?" I asked.

"That's his name," Ken said. "So, I play on two computers. Loup-garou uses his power to protect my client's character so he can gain levels."

"You're telling us that one dork out there in cyberland is paying another dork—you—to play a game for him?" Jeremy said.

"That would be the deal," Ken said. "I can make three to five hundred dollars this weekend if I play pretty much around the clock. And I'm getting a hundred bucks for twinking a guy."

The silence then was embarrassingly loud.

"Twinking. A guy?" Jeremy said.

"That sounds repulsively sexual, but since it's you, Ken, I know it can't be," I said. "You've never come close to twinking either sex."

Ken sighed, obviously disgusted with us. "Twinking is giving a weapon that only a high-level character could afford to a low-level character."

He looked back at his computer. "And I have, indeed, had sexual contact with a girl."

We didn't say anything.

"A kiss," he said.

We said nothing for a while longer.

"On the cheek, cousin, we were ten, parents thought it was a cute picture under the mistletoe." He cricked his neck around. "Like you two goons have done any better."

Jeremy, thankfully, changed the subject.

"Let me get this straight," he said. "You'd rather be a virtual hero than drink until you puke with college guys?"

Katy

I drove Katy and Morgan home from their soccer game.

"He was there again," Morgan said.

"I didn't see him," Katy said.

"I'm telling you the dude is stalking me." Morgan made a snarly face.

"Too true," Katy said. "He looks like somebody's grandfather or something."

My ears perked. Was some old perv hanging around the soccer field?

"What's going on?"

Katy sighed. Big. Dramatic. "Morgan thinks she has a stalker. This guy, who's got to be, like forty, was at soccer practice last week and he was at the game today." Katy paused. "At least Morgan says he was."

"He was so. Not for the whole game. Just for about fifteen minutes. I saw him." She whomped Katy on the shoulder.

"Anyway, she's so conceited she thinks he's watching her. I think he's the coach's boyfriend or something."

"Hey, I got two hang-up calls. You were there. That's weird, right?" Morgan seemed pleased about her stalker.

"Big deal. We've gotten a bunch, too. Got one this morning," Katy said.

"We've been getting hang-ups?"

"Sure. No big. I just hang back up."

I didn't like it. But I wondered if our hang-ups might be Skye.

"Tell your coach about this. She should know who he is. Strange men do not have a good reason to prowl around a girls' athletic field."

Morgan sobered up. "You think he could be like a serial killer or something?"

"I doubt it, but tell your coach if it happens again. Then at least you can find out if she has a new boyfriend."

"Eeewww," Katy groaned. "Coach doesn't shave her pits. Just the idea of a boyfriend. Gross."

Wanna-be Frat Guy

Jeremy and I packed what we surmised was a Joe College wardrobe and headed for Austin after Friday's last bell.

Brad's apartment was all we ever dreamed of cast-off cool. Totally testosterone with not a whiff of a mother figure. Manly heaven. We snarfed great Tex Mex and lapped up Coronas with lime on the Strip, and generally cruised and gawked until after ten, when Brad drove us to the frat house.

"Be prepared, dudes. Here's where you find out that you can leave high school behind. This is a whole 'nother enchilada."

He was right.

There were a few jocks in the frat, but not many. It seemed that jocks ruled their own sweaty world but didn't have much clout in other areas. There were geeks in every frat—the fraternity needed their GPAs. There were the rich and connected. The fraternity needed—well, their money and their connections. And the big wonder—there were dozens of guys just like Jeremy and me. Guys that got to come out of the shadows.

One of them corralled Jeremy and me. "Don't you

get it?" Richard asked. "There's lots of us in every high school—hard to count us, since we stayed so low-key. With good reason, sure. But here, the rules are changed. We find all the other nobodies and we get a chance to be somebodies."

Jeremy and I stared at Richard. "Yeah, I hear you," he said. "But there's no steroid-fueled Big Foot here shoving you headfirst into a toilet. There's no one interested in banging your face into a locker." He laughed. "Hell, there's no lockers. And there's nobody that comes to class with a hard-on and a gun."

He gestured toward us with his beer. "And the turds that won all the popularity contests and ran the school, they get pretty damn humble when they find out that there's hundreds of schools emptying them into the same big pot. The place is too big for any one group to have much power."

Richard waved to someone behind us. "Gotta go. But, guys, welcome to your new and improved world."

And so we partied. And didn't care who saw us. We talked loud, we got sloshingly drunk, and we got humblingly sick. We were part of something. I felt myself pushing at the sides of my box. Wanting out. Feeling like it might be time. Nothing had ever felt quite so fine.

Driving back on Sunday with throbbing heads and cotton-mouths, Jeremy and I decided that stopping drinking before the puking point might be good.

"Matt, if we can get through seven more months in

that hellhole, we graduate. I can see a light at the end of the tunnel, and this time it might not be the train."

"We can do seven months. We've almost done four years," I said.

Skye

When I got to the house, there were two notes from my mom. "Some girl called, she was crying." And the other, "Same girl, she's upgraded to hysterical. Is there something you want to tell me?"

I hit the computer and found seventeen e-mails from Skye. All in the I-need-to-see-you-now category. I posted her. "I'm here. What's so important?"

She IM'ed me. She must have been lurking in cyberspace.

Pick me up in an hour, I'll be waiting on the porch.

I hooked it over there and she climbed in the car. No makeup. She was pretty without all the black Goth stuff. Vulnerable. I could see that she had been crying. She waved a key. "Pirate Beach. It's a house my stepdad is fixing up, but he won't be there."

I headed toward Galveston, and Skye curled into herself and didn't speak, except to give directions. We arrived at the scruffy beach house and Skye let us in with the key. The October day was cool and misty. The place was semi-furnished, and she led me straight to the bed and slid under the covers. I slipped in beside her and pulled her against me.

"What's going on?"

"Back-story first, so you'll get the whole picture."

I nodded and settled her closer. She was trembling and I found myself rubbing her arms and back.

"Lisa is Mom and Lex's kid. They blame me for her problems. Lex says that Mom was wigged all during her pregnancy by my 'stuff.' I admit I was a bitch and a half, but I don't think stress causes Down's." She punched the pillow. "Try telling Lex."

I murmured comforting sounds.

"And Mom believes every word he says. She blames me, too."

She rolled up so she could see me as she spoke. "The deal is, I don't care what Mom or Lex think. It doesn't make any diff. They're just the people I live with, you know?"

I had some idea.

"But Lisa. Lisa loves me. She needs me and I love her. I take care of her every minute I'm not in school and if she's sick and needs me, school can just piss off."

This was all kind of interesting, but I wondered where it was going.

"Mom and Lex are, like, embarrassed about Lisa, and yesterday they took her to a state hospital and had her institutionalized." She stopped, put her hands over her face, then wiped her eyes. Her voice was low and soft as she stared down into the mattress. "They just gave her away to people that don't give a rat's ass about her."

This was bad.

"And I can't do a thing about it. Unless they die or something, I have no say. I'm not a legal guardian." She stretched out alongside me again.

I thought there was some legal fallacy in there somewhere, but Skye's hands were roaming my body now and I couldn't concentrate.

"I guess I should be glad she's there. At least Lex can't get at her."

Time stopped and all the color in the room faded to gray.

"What's that mean?"

Skye sighed and lay back against the pillow. She gripped my hand tight. "Do you think I got this messed up without a reason?"

I didn't want to hear what was coming next.

"Lex has been 'at' me since I was twelve. It's still happening."

I couldn't breathe.

"My mother knows, but I suppose she thinks it's a small price to pay. She'll ignore what Lex is doing to me just so she can stay in her house and have her car and not have to work."

Something went hard and hot in my chest. I hated these people. People who had thrown away not one child but two.

Skye sobbed. Deep, dismal cries.

She kissed me then, long and deep. She breathed her pain down into me, waking a fire of rage. She ran her hands under my shirt. "Do you have one?"

I knew exactly what she meant. There had been a condom in my wallet since I was fifteen. Waiting for me to grow into it, I guess.

I stopped her. "Yes, I've got one. But you're hurt and lonely. Having sex with you now would be . . . wrong."

"No," she whispered. "No, I need to feel something good. I need to know we're connected."

I let it happen.

With the sound of waves outside, the bed seemed like our own Gulf and we were swimmers. Front to front, our bodies slicked with sweat, each swimming and stroking, one against the other. We rode the waves to the crests, then plummeted down, only to ride the wave to the next breaker. We swam against the current that threatened to pull us under.

She slept after, and I watched her clean, naked face. She wasn't even wearing the earrings. My first attempt at lovemaking must have awakened something in me because I have never felt so . . . tender toward a person. She was as fragile as a week-old kitten. I didn't know how to help her—but I knew I had to do something.

When she woke, she smiled. Tiny and rueful. "I feel better. Not so alone."

I kissed her. "You're not alone. I'll do anything for you."

She smiled again. This time like I had given her a prize.

—

Skye went on a self-destructive rampage after that. She was caught smoking in the restrooms. She got into a confrontation with a teacher, then stalked out of the room and off the campus. She slapped a cheerleader. She got caught shoplifting at the mall.

Her world was nothing but hurt. Her sister was gone, her mother was sacrificing her to Lex's perversions . . . what else could she do but act out her rage so someone would get a clue?

Parents

"So, who's the girl that called crying last week?"

Mom ladled soup into my bowl. It was a rare occasion when Mom was home for supper. My mother is a party favor. That's what I called her when I was kid. Actually, she's a professional party giver. She gives whoop-de-doos for corporations, businesses, fundraisers held by people with lots of money. Most of the parties are on weekends and evenings.

I find it mildly ironic that Mom gives parties, and since sixth grade, I haven't been invited to any. In elementary school, the mark of success was how many tykes attended your party. Starting in middle school, the idea of a party was exclusionary. No dweebs, nerds, or nobodies allowed.

Katy sometimes helped with parties. But I embarrassed Mom the few times I accompanied her. I skulked in shadows and couldn't make neither chit nor chat. So I was left to amuse myself at home, to become the Rerun King.

"What girl?" asked Dad. He's a tax lawyer for a major corporation. He works lots of hours at his office and comes home to work more hours.

"Some girl called Matt twice last weekend. She was crying and hysterical."

Dad's eyebrows went up. He looked completely lame.

"Relax, there has been no impregnation on my part of anyone I know."

"Shit!" Katy's exclamation was sort of a bark. Her smile quickly turned to her "oops" face at Mom's scowl. My mother and father don't like profanity. A lot.

"Sorry, Mom. It just kind of jumped out of me." She hiked up her shoulders.

I did my big brother duty and leapt to her aid. "Tourette's? You should have her checked, Mom. Really."

Mom scowled more, but Dad appeared too relieved at my denial of paternity to mind.

I continued to keep Mom off Katy's back and both of them off mine. "She's someone that's flunking and was desperate for some help. We had a test Monday. I met with her when I got back from Austin and helped her out."

"That was nice of you, Matt."

My parents were a continuing mystery. My mother had had an affair. They were lying to Katy and to me about Katy's father. About each other. They lived a lie. Why couldn't they recognize one?

Skye

Skye cooled out for a while. We saw each other at the park, at the beach house. I thought I was her cure. I thought if I loved her without question, I might be able to help her.

One evening we drove to the ferry that runs from Galveston to Bolivar. We parked the car and walked on, going up to the highest railing at the prow. She stood in front of me, my arms wrapped around her, her weight against me, sweet and warm. We watched the sun sinking into the horizon and didn't say much.

"My mother taught me purple," she said.

My mind went immediately to bruises.

She leaned sideways to see my face, closed her eyes and shook her head, then slid back, resting the back of her head against my shoulder. "No. She didn't beat me. Not all my memories are bad, you know."

I didn't know.

"It was during one of her temporary cleanups, I guess. I was little."

She quieted and I waited.

She sighed. "Maybe it was before she ever gave me away. I'm not sure."

Silence again. Something niggled at my mind. A what's-wrong-with-this-picture thing. But her body was resting easily against me. No tension. I shoved the unformed thought away.

"I think I was just learning the colors, the names of them, you know? And I remember we lived in an old house, not an apartment, and it was a wreck. It was evening, and Mom held me up to see out the window. The pane was cracked and the sill was broken off, but the sunset was amazing. Mom said, 'Look, Skye, that's purple.'"

Skye pointed to the stripe of color just above the horizon. "It was that color. Not a wimpy lavender or too much blue so it looks bruised, but that color."

The rich, deep purple glowed; then the sun sank more and it darkened.

"It never stays long," she said.

We were at the beach house, sitting on the porch. We wrapped up in one blanket and shared a bag of Chips Ahoy. I had seen Skye with a camera a few times at school and I had finally asked her about it. She brought a ring binder with her that I was leafing through.

It contained digital photos printed on copy paper. Like Skye herself, they weren't normal. There was a series of ear shots. Ears. Twenty or more. Little ones, big ones, pierced and multi-pierced, all kinds of ears. And a series of noses, eyebrows, bald heads, followed by a series of what looked like really bad toupees. Could have been roadkill. Some pictures showed whole faces. Faces that were angry, sullen, or just blank. All were of people. None were of me.

I closed the binder and handed it back. She replaced it in her backpack.

"No comment?" she asked.

Okay, there couldn't be pics of me if I had to be a secret, but I still felt left out.

"Skye, what's the deal with the shoplifting? I can get on board with screwing with the shrink, I wouldn't want a stranger rooting around in my private thoughts either, but why get in trouble with the law?"

"Why not?" she said. "It was a great jacket. Very biker chick."

"But why steal it?"

She gave me the look that said even a toad should understand. "It was there. I wanted it. End of story." Skye dug around in her jeans and produced a joint. "Ya want?"

"Sure," I said. I plucked it from her fingers and pitched it over the railing. It landed in a puddle left by the high tide.

She flung off the blanket and sailed down the steps, retrieving the soggy joint.

"That's just great!" she screamed up at me. "Even if I dry it out, it's got saltwater in it." She stormed up the steps and into the house.

She came back out with my keys. "Dickhead." She started back down the stairs. I lunged for her ankle, and caught it. She whirled around and kicked me dead in the chest. I let go of the ankle and she bolted for the car and drove away.

In my car.

I waited for over an hour, but she didn't come back.

I had to walk a couple of miles to a pay phone. I started to call Jeremy, then wondered how the hell I could explain why I was at Pirate Beach without my car.

I leaned against the pay phone, cursing Skye and wondering what to do, when inspiration struck. I dialed information and got the number. She answered on the second ring.

Taylor

"Taylor?"

"Yes."

"This is, um, Matt Lathrop. You know who I am?"

"Sure, you're the guy that doesn't believe in conversation."

I rubbed my forehead and wondered if I could hitchhike back home. "Yep, that would be me. You said that we could talk about Skye if I wanted, remember?"

"What's she done?"

"It's a little complicated," I said, hoping that wasn't a hint of a whine I heard in my voice.

"We're talking about Skye. Complicated is an understatement."

"The problem is I'm in Galveston and Skye got mad and sort of took off in my car."

Taylor sighed. "Why call me? Don't you have friends that can pick you up?"

I didn't know what to say. I scuffed my sneaker in the sand and thumped around a little.

"Matt?"

"Yeah, I have a friend or two, but I can't call them. I would have to tell them about Skye."

"Where are you?"

Taylor arrived and I slumped into her car. "Thanks," I said. "It's a long walk back."

"Sure, and by the way, I drove past Skye's. Your car's parked about two doors down from hers. Keys were in the ignition, so I took them." She pointed to the glove compartment.

I retrieved them. "Why do they call them glove compartments? Did anyone in history actually keep gloves in there?"

"Avoiding the subject much?"

"Fine," I said. "But tell me how you connected me and Skye. You just saw us talking once. And how do you know my car?"

Taylor shrugged, and that great hair shivered on her shoulders. "I know your car because I watched you park once. I wanted to see if you brought Skye to school. I know Skye. She's a predator, and I could tell she had found prey."

That pissed me off. "She's not a predator. In fact, it's more the other way around."

"Have it your way—but how come you're in my car and not your own?"

That pissed me off more. Taylor had overlooked my hero-ness and zoned in on the stupid.

"Look," Taylor said. "You're not ready to talk about Skye yet. If you were, you wouldn't be keeping her a secret. I'll be glad to keep this 'incident' to myself. When it all comes apart, you're going to need a few facts. Skye has lots of problems."

I was still playing defense. "Yeah, maybe she does. But if you had a stepfather like hers, you'd have problems, too."

Taylor slowed down and turned to look at me. "Stepfather? Skye doesn't have a stepfather."

I didn't, couldn't say anything. I pulled at my eyelashes. Finally, "Skye told me that Lex is her stepfather."

All Taylor had to say to that was, "Oh."

"How do you know so much about Skye, anyway?"

Taylor turned the radio off. "She moved here the same year I did. When we were twelve. Both new girls, you know? Everybody else already had friends, so we kind of drifted together."

"And?"

"And for about a year we were best friends." Taylor tapped the steering wheel. Her nails were short, with no polish. "Well, as good as it gets with Skye, anyway," she said.

She slid a glance at me. "Do you know all about the foster homes and that her mother used to be a cokehead?"

"Used to be?" I said. "Aren't you sort of always in recovery or something?"

Taylor looked at me, her forehead wrinkled in what could only be confusion. "You're talking like her mother is alive." She turned her attention back to the road.

My head couldn't hold this story and Skye's story at the same time. And something inside my already-full head was whispering to me not to believe Taylor, and something else was telling me that I was in deep, deep shit.

"Just lay it out for me," I said. "About Skye's parents."

"Skye's mother was a doper," Taylor said. "She had Skye and dropped her with the state and wouldn't tell who Skye's father was. Skye was in and out of foster homes most of her life. Her mother got AIDS and just before she died, she gave it up. Told that Lex was Skye's father, but he didn't know anything about it."

Taylor was nearing an intersection. "I'm guessing you want me to drop you off at your car?"

I nodded, and Taylor hooked a left. "I don't know how it all works, but Mr. Colby got notified, he said he wanted Skye, and that was when she moved here and we met."

She pulled alongside my car. "What did she tell you?"

"Nothing, I must have gotten it mixed up." I stepped out. "Thanks for picking me up." I closed the door.

Taylor shook her head, her lips pressed together. It's an expression I once saw on someone who'd just seen a puppy hit by a car.

Skye

I opened my car door and found the note. A lopsided heart. Inside the heart was, "Forgive me. I need you." The writing was red and still sticky. This time it was blood.

—

At home, I went to bed without checking my e-mail. I needed to think. I didn't want to think. I was furious with Skye for stranding me. I couldn't believe I had made her bleed so she could show me how sorry she was. Why had she told one story to Taylor and another to me? I had promised myself to help Skye. God knows she needed someone. Okay, it was harder, more confusing and frustrating than I had bargained for. But people had bailed on Skye all her life.

I couldn't make any of this stuff line up. I felt like someone had tossed pieces of three or four puzzles into one box. I couldn't sleep and I didn't want to deal with this shit anymore. If I stayed awake all night, I wouldn't have any eyelashes in the morning. When I was sure Mom and Dad were down for the night, I slithered downstairs and got a bottle of JD. I'd drink myself to sleep.

Some godawful racket woke me. My head split open and my stomach lurched. I barely made it to the toilet. I gakked and yarked and my head cracked more. Finally empty, I rinsed out my mouth and staggered back to bed with a wet washcloth over my face.

I had done big bad and Bobo the teetotaler god was sticking it to me.

The phone rang again. This time I picked up.

"Matt? Will you talk to me?"

Skye.

"Skye, I can't handle it if you cry or argue."

"You sound funny."

"Funny, no, I don't feel anything related to funny. I'm hung in a big, big kind of over."

She didn't answer.

The silence felt good.

"And so, a joint is wrong but drinking is cool?"

I hung up on her. I'd rather she be crazy than be right.

After aspirin and a shower, I called Skye back.

"I've got an idea," I said when she answered.

"Don't call my house again. You're lucky no one else is here," she said.

"Can I talk now?"

"Talk," she said.

"I won't drink if you won't toke. You were right, both things are stupid."

I could hear her breathe, but nothing else.

"Skye, I was out of line. Your stuff belongs to you,

and I shouldn't have thrown it away. So we're even. I took your shit, you took my car."

Still nothing.

"Okay, I'll leave you alone," I said.

"Don't hang up," Skye said. "He did it again last night."

"Your father?"

Her tone was ice shards. "Stepfather."

"His name is Colby, too. That's how I found you in the phone book."

She hesitated. "Mom got him to adopt me. That way, if he ever divorces her, he still has to leave me money and she'll get child support."

"Skye, you need to tell someone. The police or the school."

"You don't get it."

"What don't I get?" I wandered around the room, kicking at furniture.

"What can I prove? Lex will lie. Mom will lie. There are quite a few guys that'll say they've had sex with me. Do you think the counselors are gonna say I'm a sweet young thing that would never tell a lie?"

She had a point there. Being known as the school whackoid didn't do much for your cred.

"He can't keep doing this," I said.

"I know." Long silence. Then her voice was a harsh whisper. "I'd rather kill myself than let him touch me again."

I didn't have an answer for her. I didn't have any answers.

"This isn't phone chat," Skye said. "I want to see you soon. I have an idea myself."

"Sure. And Skye," I said, "don't worry. I'll take care of you."

But I started keeping a chart. Of what Skye said. And the contradictions.

Skye wasn't Skye when I saw her at school Monday. She had done some self-mutilating on her hair and, instead of spikes, it was in patches and clumps. The Goth makeup was back, but before, it was almost a work of art—now it was sloppy and smeared. While her eyes were often blank before, now they were dead. I wanted to take her home and spoon-feed her soup.

But I knew better than to approach her.

I spent a fitful week. No calls, no e-mails, no notice at all from Skye. She wasn't at school Wednesday or Thursday. When she returned Friday, she didn't get kicked out, so I guess she really was sick or had joined society enough to forge her own note.

Something else arrived Friday. Flyers. By noon they were taped to lockers, stacks were left in the bathrooms, and thrown around the cafeteria tables like oversized confetti.

Ken handed me one when I sat down. A banner ran across the top of the flyer: "CAN YOU NAME THE ASS?"

Ken & Jeremy

Under the banner were ten thumbnail photos. Of butts. Feminine. In jeans, shorts, very short shorts, bikini bottoms, gym clothes, lycra bike shorts, thongs. Just the butts. No faces, no legs, not even knees. Asses only.

Ken pointed to the thong-clad fanny. "That's Ann Fields." He shifted his finger. "And that's Melissa Poland." He jabbed at the lycra-ed rump. "Jenny Sanchez." He paused on the jeans. "I'm pretty sure that's Kelley Janek."

Jeremy shook his head. "Wrong, Kelley is the gym shorts; the jeans is Lauren Vale."

"Do you know every one of these?" I asked.

"You don't?" Ken shot back.

I looked back at the flyer. Okay, yes. I didn't need to see any faces.

Ken put the flyer in his lit text. "Who did this? It's digital and the pics have been cropped. Somebody that's at least passing fair with PhotoShop did it." He scanned the cafeteria. "That takes in all the nerd herd and most of the rest—well, exclude the jocks. Most of them, anyway."

"So how did any of the geeks manage to get a picture of Ann Fields wearing butt floss?" Jeremy asked.

I don't know how she did it, but I knew who. All the pictures were of the most popular girls in school. With the exception of Taylor Banks. Skye wasn't just ferociously, sarcastically in everyone's face. She could be loyal.

—

As we left the campus, another round of flyers appeared at the bus stop, strung along the steps leading out of the building.

This banner read, "OKAY YOU KNOW THE ASSES CAN YOU PICK THE PRICKS"? Ten thumbnails again. Crotches. Mostly in jeans. A couple in football pants. One in a swim team "teeny weenie" suit. I refused to admit if I recognized even one of them.

Ken didn't keep this flyer. And while the ass flyer caused a few embarrassed giggles and lots of male chest thumping, flyer number two made its point and those flyers ended up wadded or ripped. A couple of geeks who had let people believe flyer one was fun of their making were now shouting disclaimers. There were some pissed-off asses and pricks in the audience.

Skye

At home I had an e-mail.

Pick me up at the mall.
We'll go to the beach house. 7.

I pulled into the mall parking lot and cruised past the main entrance. Leave it to Skye not to tell me where in the damned mall. I circled, figuring she'd be at a side entrance. Bingo.

She got into the car and I blurted, "Hey, it was funny, but when they figure out it's you—" She held up a hand like she was warding off evil, then rubbed her temples and grimaced. She did it again when I opened my mouth. We rode the rest of the way in silence. I knew from her face that the flyers were not a means for fun, but another run at self-destruction.

At the beach house, she sailed past the door and into the bedroom, shucked her clothes, crawled under the blanket, and held her arms out to me.

I crawled in, but kept my clothes on.

"Matt," she murmured, unbuttoning me.

"Nope, not yet. Skye, you've got to stop telling me bits and pieces of the story."

She rolled to her back and rested her forearm over her eyes.

I sat and pulled the blanket from her upper body. I had felt them before in my love-travels over her skin, but had never let myself look. The slashes. Some were healed white lines. Some were red, closed flesh, and a few were crusted with blood.

I touched a scar on the inner part of her upper arm. Another above her breast. Most of them were there. A few old ones were high on her inner thighs.

"Why?" I kept my voice kiss-soft.

I could hear the waves crashing outside and a dog barking somewhere that wasn't here.

Skye's words were hesitant but not soft. Steel wrapped in velvet. She kept her arm over her eyes.

"When I feel the cut and see the blood, then . . ."

She moved her arm and gazed at the ceiling. "Then I know I'm alive."

"You need out of there," I said. I pulled her up, against me, and kissed the crown of her head. "Is there anywhere you can go?"

Her head moved back and forth. "Nowhere."

"Could you, like, check yourself back into foster care?"

She jerked back. "And you think that stuff doesn't happen in foster care?"

I was stunned. I had never lived in Skyeworld. Was there no safe place?

"You could take off. I have some bank. I'll give it to you."

She dropped back against the mattress and cradled her head with her hand. The motion lifted her breasts up. God, I hated myself for noticing.

"You certainly seem in a hurry to get me gone."

"No, no," I said, rolling down beside her and kissing one cheek, while I soothed the other with my fingertips. "I don't want you gone. I want you safe."

"Safe," she breathed. "What does that feel like?"

I wrapped my arms around her. "Like this."

No response.

"I've run before," she said.

I waited.

"Three times. I always get found."

I could imagine that. The girl was entirely too visible.

"There's only one way out of this," she said.

I waited some more.

"Death," Skye said. "His or mine."

Katy

It was late-thirty when I got home, but Katy was in front of my computer when I came in—frazzled. I didn't mind Katy's using my computer, but I would be glad when I got my agreed-upon graduation laptop and the desktop could be moved to Katy's room.

I leaned over her shoulder to see two cybergirls yanking out each other's hair. Katy was typing insults that appeared onscreen.

"Whoa, Katydidn't. What are you doing?" Maybe she was power-leveling, too.

"It's called Bitch Slap," bullfrog-voiced Katy said. "When you're ready to go physical on somebody, you play this game instead. You create your virtual enemy and bitch-slap her around. It's monitored, though. No cussing."

I flopped on the bed.

"I guess I have to disappear." Katy banged the return key with a satisfied wallop.

"The game could do with the disappearing, but could we talk?"

She closed down the file, then laced her fingers behind her head, stretched out her legs, and said in an accent so bad I couldn't figure out what it was supposed to be, "And how long have you been haffing these thoughts about haffing sex with weasels?"

Even with all my circuits fried, she made me laugh. Where would I be without Katy? My lifeline to sanity. I threw a pillow at her. She let it hit her and didn't move.

"Yaz, yaz. Always, wif the denial. That's the first phase, you see."

She picked up the pillow and fired it back. "What's up big bro of mine?"

"First, there's a few rules," I said.

Katy tilted her head and put her hands to the side, palms up, in the "As if I didn't know that" expression.

"This stays here, there's questions I won't answer, and it's serious, so don't mess with me too much."

Katy hiked her eyebrows; then her face slid into solemn mode. "Gimme one of the pillows," she said. She sat on the bed facing me, squished the pillow behind her back at the footboard. "Start talking."

"We know that I pretty much don't trust a lot of—"

"You don't trust anyone. Well, maybe me. Why is that, exactly?"

"Another time." Sure, two minutes after my ass learned to chew gum. "Keeping in mind my lack-of-trust issue, there is a person—" Katy opened her mouth. I held up a finger. "Who shall remain nameless. This . . ." I paused, sighed, looked around the room. "This person told me some things. Bad things. Things that this person is . . . um, victim to."

"How bad?" Katy asked. "Report-to-the-police bad?"

I nodded.

We waited each other out.

"And you haven't reported it yourself because . . .?"

I banged my head softly against the headboard. My eyes roamed the room and finally lit on Katy. "I guess I'm not totally sure I believe everything." I sighed. "Maybe some. But not all of it."

Katy kind of puckered her mouth up and knotted her eyebrows. "And, you're trying to figure out if this is Matt paranoia or would a normal, sane person be suspicious?"

"Right."

Katy settled back against the pillow. "I need data."

"This person is kind of 'out there.'"

Katy raised her hand to high-five me. "Matt, my Matt, running with something outside the nerd herd? Congrats!"

I arched my evil eyebrow and ignored her hand. "This person sometimes does drugs, gets in trouble at school, and lies to get out of trouble."

Katy arched her evil eyebrow.

"According to this person, the living arrangement is a sister, a mother, and a stepfather."

"Okay," Katy said, sounding not okay at all.

"But this person told someone else that the family consisted of a stepmother and a father."

Katy sank deeper into the pillow. "Wow."

"I caught a flaw in this person's story once. Something about foster homes, when this person first went into the system. It could be explained, I guess, but—"

"Matt, see this?" Katy held up both hands, fingers extending and pulsing in and out. "That's bullshit radar—and it's in hyperdrive."

"You think this person is lying," I said.

She ticked things off on her fingers. "Drugs, stealing, school trouble, lies elsewhere, has trouble remembering who birthed 'this person,' and most important—you won't tell me who 'this person' is, won't let me meet 'this person.' Add that all up and I think 'this person' is a big problem."

"So, what should I do?" I asked.

Katy stood up. She pulled down her T-shirt and smoothed her jeans. Only then did she look at me.

"Matt, I'm thirteen years old."

She stared at me as if that should be enough. When I didn't respond, she sighed, clearly frustrated.

"This is serious stuff. I can't tell you anything. You should be talking to a grown-up."

She left, but not before she looked at me, for the first time, like I had disappointed her.

Wanna-be Frat Guy

The next day, Jeremy's brother came home with Richard, his frat brother, in tow. We grabbed Ken and hit Houston and the bars on Westheimer. Since Brad was a Phi Delt, Jeremy pretty much had a bid locked, but Richard seemed to be scouting Ken and me. A good frat pledge button on my shirt seemed attainable by the time we had made it into and were thrown out of a couple of titty bars. I kept my alcohol consumption at the level called moderate. That wasn't exactly what I'd agreed to with Skye—but hell, I knew Skye lied. Maybe she wouldn't toke, but most of her drug use was pharmaceutical anyway.

It was owl time when I got into my bed, and my head was still revving. I was putting myself in two worlds here. The wild world of weird, and prep-boy world. The two couldn't merge. I didn't want to give up Skye. I liked playing my savior role. And I liked the sex. But, being able to walk in the real world—that was something I had always wanted. Needed. I needed normal. Skye needed me. But she wasn't and would never be anything close to normal. I couldn't have both.

Didn't Hamlet have a problem like that?

Sunday, I found e-mail from Skye. She'd been e-ing me since last night. The morning posts were full of hostility, telling me that I hadn't been there for her when she needed me.

I ignored them and I didn't know why.

Monday, Skye wore baggy sweatpants, a short-sleeved tee, and a long, fresh cut from elbow to wrist. Her homeroom teacher whisked her to the office, the office got her to the school counselor/shrink, her mother was contacted and so was social services. Ken's sister works in the office for her first class, so the 411 was reliable. Skye was back in the system.

She didn't come back for two weeks. I heard nothing. Richard called me from UT asking about my GPA, my ability to pay frat dues, and my feelings about early rush. It was easier thinking about that than about Skyestuff.

The word came down that Skye had been hospitalized for psychiatric evaluation. Her family was being evaluated by social services. Surely, they'd find out if her dad/stepdad/whatever was a perv. I was pretty much convinced by now that he wasn't. But the shrink would help Skye learn to fly in formation with the other birds. I could have her and the real world.

Sure.

The note in my locker said, "Park, 9."

I considered not going.

She was there before me. On our bench. Swaying.

She held out her forearm. The cut was nearly healed. "This was because of you, not him."

I sighed. "Why? What did I do?"

"You weren't there."

I strode past her, tore a handful of leaves from the weeping willow, and stared at the bayou. "I didn't know I was supposed to be on call."

I turned to see tears chasing each other down her cheeks. Her expression wasn't connected to the tears. "I know," she said, voice flat. "But I just . . . I . . ."

I went to her, pulled her up, and wrapped her in my arms. What need did she have that was so deep that she would lie and drug and steal to escape? How could she be so fierce one minute and so broken now?

"I can't live like this anymore," she said.

"I'll help," I said. "I'll do whatever you need."

Skye pulled back, put her cold hands on my cheeks. "Do you mean that?"

I kissed her. "I'll do whatever you want."

She kissed me, light, delicate, a haunting ghost-kiss, then swayed into me and kissed me deep, breathing her Skyeness into me. How could I have ever thought of leaving her?

Her mouth traveled up to my ear. "Kill my parents. Kill them for me."

Her words turned me into statueman. I couldn't breathe, think, feel, move. Skye was still in my arms, her mouth next to my ear. She said it again. "Kill my parents, Matt. It's what I need. It's the only way."

I peeled her off me and held my hands out. "Whoa."

She looked so delicate, so vulnerable. She couldn't mean this.

"Skye, you're either under- or overmedicated. Let's go home and forget this. You'll feel better—"

"I'll never feel better. Not until they're dead. Lex is home boozing. Do you know what that means for me? My sister is in an institution and she'll be there forever unless I become her guardian. And I can't do that if either of them are alive." Her eyes weren't blank anymore. They were cold fire, burning with drugs and hatred.

"I can't. I won't." I shook my head. "Shit, Skye, I wouldn't even know how."

She slithered in close and took my hand, pulling us both down on the bench. "I know how. I've planned it all out."

She put her head on my thigh just as she had that first night. And I remembered something. I picked you out, she had said. I picked you out.

"Lex has a gun. It's in the top of the hall closet and he probably doesn't even remember it's there. When things look right for it, I'll cut myself bad and go to the hospital. The next night, while I'm still there, you wait until they go to sleep. Go in, shoot Lex first, in the right temple, then shoot Mom, wherever, as long as it kills her. Then press Lex's fingers to the gun, drop it on the bed with them, and leave. No one, but no one, would ever suspect you. There's no reason for anyone to link you and me."

I picked you out. I picked you out. Ipickedyouout.

I shoved Skye off me. "You planned this from the jump," I said. "You picked the guy nobody sees, pulled me in with sex, kept us a secret—all so I could murder your parents?"

She smiled. That rueful smile that had touched my heart. Bound me to her. I wanted to slap it off her face. Blood roared in my ears. I pressed my fists against my jeans. I wouldn't hit her. I wouldn't.

Jeremy

I blazed to Jeremy's.

"Hey, dude, don't knock it down," he said as he pulled open the door. "What's with the Big Bad Wolf routine?"

"Sorry," I said. "Don't know my own strength." I made a muscleman arm.

"You can't fool Joltin' Jeremy; you were poundin' on that door with your head."

Jeremy pointed to the kitchen, then upstairs. Translation: Parents awake upstairs, keep voice down, we can talk in the kitchen.

I straddled a chair and took the Coke Jeremy shoved my way.

"Let's get out of town," I said. "Go see Brad, go camping, beam our way to Mars."

"Wow, that must have been a 'palooza fight," Jeremy said.

"Huh?" How could he know about Skye, much less about our fight?

"Yeah, was it your dad, your mom, or did they double-team you?" Jeremy popped the tab on his Mountain

Dew. "Gotta be a gang bang. You wouldn't want to leave town if it was just one."

Saved.

From what? Why didn't I tell Jeremy about Skye? Why didn't I go home and tell my parents? Katy?

Because I would have to admit, right out loud, that I was stupid enough to believe that a girl like Skye, a sex-walking force-of-nature female, would want me. That it had never entered my mind that she was using me. I was pathetic and didn't want anyone else to know how deep the pathetic ran.

"Camping," Jeremy went on. Did I need to be in the room? "We haven't been camping since Cub Scouts. Nope, no can do. Didn't like bugs then, don't like 'em now. Mars." Jeremy raised a finger as if evaluating. "Mars. Good option. Like it. Can you do the math? All that light-year stuff? We'd need to figure out if we can get back for class on Monday."

Obviously, I didn't need to be in the room. Now Jeremy couldn't even see me.

"Last option is my beloved brother Bradley. That would be problematic."

"Why?"

"'Cause he's not in Austin."

"Shit." I was reduced to one-word sentences with Jeremy in the room.

"But he is in a beach house at Surfside."

"Huh?"

"Yep, he popped in on his way there. Since it's

November and rates are"—his hand dived—"down. He and his band of bros decided to party off campus." He grinned. "He said that my band of bros are invited."

"Your band of bros? You have a pretty limited band." Look at me—multisyllabic.

"Elite. I prefer, elite. Small sounds so . . . well, small."

"Cool," I said.

"Absolutely fuckin' cool," Jeremy said. "They barbeque at one and party until Sunday afternoon."

That worked for me.

"So which parental authority figure is giving you shit-fits?"

"Huh?" I said. It was a monosyllabic, multiuse kind of word. I liked it.

Then I homed in. "Oh, neither one. I've just got the major wig going on."

Jeremy nodded, all sage and wise man. "I know the feeling."

He didn't know this feeling. I don't think he had ever had a ladylove who asked him to play Terminator.

I hung with Jeremy a while and got home late. Mom was still party pushing and Dad was down for the count. I unplugged my computer and my phone. I thought I'd never sleep. But I zoned as soon as my head hit the pillow.

Wanna-be Frat Guy

Saturday was misty and cold. Ken picked up Jeremy and then me. Crappy weather is not sufficient reason for frat men to cancel a party. A makeshift tent swayed over the barbecue pit; the beer and the plates were in the screened section under the beach house. Everyone was in jeans and light jackets. Even Taylor Banks.

Taylor

"Grab us a couple of beers and meet me on the porch," she said.

I chatted and smiled as I made my way to the cooler. I saw Ann Fields, who didn't seem to see me. Some other girls and a couple of guys from high school milled around. Looks like the frat was trawling the locals who would be going to UT.

Taylor was on the top step, just outside the porch.

"Too much noise in there," she said, taking her beer.

"What's your connection here?" I asked.

"My older sister dates a Phi Delt. She's a Kappa."

"Got it. I'm here because Jeremy's brother Brad—"

"Is a Phi Delt, I know."

Of course she would. She knew people. She was Taylor Banks. Taylor Banks always parties with the coolest of the cool.

"Still with Skye?"

I drank my beer.

Taylor. "Say no more. I've been there."

"I doubt you've been where I am," I said.

Taylor wrinkled her nose.

"I didn't mean that sexually," I said. "I'm so hopeless."

"I meant," Taylor said, "that I know how Skye can go too far and I'd tell myself I'd never hang with her again. Then somehow, she pulled my string. Face it, if there's no excitement, Skye manufactures some."

I nodded. Conversation with sane girls was something I couldn't handle. I allowed myself a half smile. Skye manufactured excitement? Oh, yes, she wore a sheen of excitement on her skin like most people had sweat.

"Did she try to float the dead twin story past you?"

"Dead twin? No. Does she have a dead twin?" My head shouted, Did she ask someone to kill her twin?

"Who the hell knows?" Taylor said. "Skye says that Lex doesn't even know she had a twin, so I couldn't ask him." She arched her brow and quirked one side of her mouth, demonstrating her suspicion, I guess. "She told me that her twin died when they were like two or something. She said that the twin was named Stormy and she was named Skye, so she used the names together sometimes." Taylor rolled her eyes and sighed. "And . . . she says her twin still talks to her in a twinspeak language thingy." Taylor took a drink. "Major weird."

I pulled hard at my beer. "What ripped it for you?" I asked. "With Skye."

Taylor sighed. "Understand something. I'm not trying to be all-knowing or Miss Together. My dad is a psychiatrist, but my mother is the person I talk to. Go to for help." She smiled, sort of to herself. Then she looked up at me. "Mom guided me through the Skye thing, and I guess I'm trying to return the favor with you." She sighed. "Like my Grandma would say, 'Hells bells.'" She pushed her hair behind her ear. "Look at Skye pulling me back into her web." She looked at me again. "I don't want to hurt your feelings, but I don't think you're . . . savvy enough for Skye. You're kind of reactive, rather than active. Skye locks in on that. And the other thing is that you're nice."

"Nice," I said. Who calls a guy "nice"? Same girl that says "hells bells," I guess.

Taylor smiled and patted my knee. "It's a compliment. Honest. I want to help you if I can, but you'll tell me if I step on your toes?"

"You got it," I said.

"In eighth grade, Skye had Ms. Elworth for history."

"We called her—"

"Smellsfish," we said together.

"Because she always had her face pinched up like she smelled bad fish," Taylor said.

I nodded. "I had her, too. She was young to be that mean. I thought it took a while, you know?"

Taylor nodded. "Smellsfish hated Skye, and Skye did all kinds of stuff just to jerk her around."

"That's hard to imagine," I said, going for cool, sarcastic guy. Not nice guy. Nope, not that.

"Skye was failing history, and if that happened, she'd have to repeat eighth grade." Taylor put her beer on the step below us. "Skye and I hadn't been hanging together much, but she knew that I baby-sat for Smellsfish sometimes. She also knew that Smellsfish didn't keep her grades on the computer. She was the old-fashioned kind—grades in the black grade book with the green lined paper."

"They still make those things?"

Taylor shrugged. "Skye got all friendly again, didn't step out of bounds much." Taylor stopped. "I hate saying this, but I was overweight then, didn't get . . ." she trailed off. "Decent looking until ninth grade, so I didn't have many friends to pick from."

"You made up for lost time," I said. I meant it as a compliment, but Taylor flinched.

"I didn't mean that to sound stuck on myself," she said.

Revelation. Taylor was embarrassed. She was not all confident and self-assured as I'd thought.

She waved her fingers in front of my eyes. "Back to earth, Matt?"

"Right."

Taylor continued, but she didn't look at me now. The knees of her jeans had suddenly become interesting. "We hung out for a couple of weeks, and then Skye asked if Smellsfish took her grade book home on weekends."

I felt it coming.

"To get to the end of this story, before we get old, Skye got me to steal the grade book."

"You did it?"

"I did. I figured that, without Smellsfish's grades,

everyone would pass and there was no bad."

"Did it work?" I asked.

"Sure did."

"And?" I said. "I feel an 'and.'"

"And," Taylor said, "the last day of school, well, that night, Skye took the grade book to Smellsfish's house and set fire to it on her lawn."

Oh.

"I told my mom. We talked to the principal and the police, but there was no proof. I didn't see her do it. I just knew she did." Taylor hooked her hair behind the other ear, and when she sighed it seemed to deflate her.

"Ms. Elworth didn't come back to teaching after that, and she never had me baby-sit again." Taylor turned back to me. "Skye wants what she wants—and most of the time what she wants is revenge. And she uses other people to get it."

I nodded.

"Mom and Dad showed me that Skye needed help, but that I couldn't, shouldn't be the one to help her. And that Skye only sees people for their usefulness."

I shivered, suddenly cold.

"As for all the stories, the twin thing, the stepfather/father thing, that's just Skye reinventing herself." Taylor pointed to the clone people around the barbeque pit. "And isn't that what we're doing here? Trying on our different selves."

Taylor stood. "There's one more thing," she said. "Something my mom told me. 'Don't love something that can't love you back.'" She stepped past me, then looked over her shoulder.

"And Matt, Skye can't love anybody."

Skye

A new thought elbowed in. Sure, I knew Skye didn't love me. According to Taylor, she couldn't love anyone. But was there something else? Did I love Skye? Or did I love who I was when I was with her?

And yes, Skye certainly used people, and I was the usee of choice for now. I had opened the door with the "I'll do anything for you" white-knight, romance-novel-stud bullshit. Nobody sane asks her boyfriend to kill her parents. Okay, maybe in those bad made-for-chicks cable movies, but that's not real life. Was Skye testing me?

Was her sense of safety so screwed up that she needed me to make a promise that dramatic to prove myself?

Or was it real? Did Skye connect so deeply with the fate of her little sister, her half sister, who had been dumped into the state's care system, that she did mean it? Would Skye kill to protect her sister?

If Katy and I lived in Skye's world, would I kill to protect Katy?

Wanna-be Frat Guy

I put the whole Skye movie on pause and enjoyed the party. Ann Fields got drunk, and I saw her disappear with three different frat boys during the course of the night. But Ann Fields wouldn't be called slut—or slute, either. It didn't work that way.

Brad introduced me to all his frat brothers.

I worked on my temperance pledge and nursed two beers the entire time. Ate the burgers that were burned on the edges and raw in the center with fake gusto. A booze-filled college girl sat in my lap and nuzzled my neck while she slurred that I was "cute as one of those Teddy Bear hamsters." She didn't ignite me the way Skye did, but hey, she was a college woman. I tried to be witty, cool, and non-nerd.

A new Matt.

New Matt

I got home Sunday afternoon feeling like I had choices. A new concept. I crashed on my carefully made bed, still in sneakers and windbreaker, and slept until Monday morning.

Katy

"Are you in there?"

Katy had pried up one eyelid and was peering in. I batted her hand away.

"Get lost, Katydidn't."

"You'll be late for school."

"Big whoop."

"Mom and Dad might not care, but as for me . . ." Katy did a fake Latin accent, "You got some 'splainin' to do, Lucy." I heard a car horn. "That's Morgan. I have to go."

I rolled over and slept for another thirty minutes, and for the first time ever, I was late to class. I hit the corridor after I got the "it's a personal insult to me when you are tardy" reprimand from the teacher—and collided with Taylor.

Taylor

Taylor looked at the ground when she spoke. “She’s in the hospital again. This time it was bad. Overdose.”

I staggered to my locker. I pressed my forehead against the cool metal. It’s him or me, himormehimorme filled my head to bursting. I wouldn’t kill her demon, and Skye decided to escape another way. I dumped my books and headed for my car.

Skye

A woman who looked as comfortable as an overstuffed chair sat at the information desk.

"Skye Colby?" I asked.

Becki, definitely with an I, as I read on her badge, typed like her fingers were embedded in molasses. "Five thirty-six," she said, peering at me over her half glasses.

▬

I stood in front of the door, then shoved my way in. She was curled on her side, away from me. I waited, wondering whether to wake her.

"I don't want breakfast, or lunch, or whatever you're offering." Skye's voice was toneless and small. A shiver rather than a shake.

"It's me," I said.

"Oh." Nothing that spoke hope, just a release of breath. "Me? I don't like me."

Was this Skyespeak or was she finally telling the truth?

I crossed the room and perched on the edge of an aluminum-legged, plastic-seat chair that faced her. "I don't like me much, either," I said. "And people wonder why I'm not popular."

She was more than pale; she seemed drained, her lips a cross between gray and purple. Dusty lavender, maybe. A shade possibly preferred by vampires, but unbecoming on the living. Her eyes were dull, her face slack and expressionless.

I reached out and took her hand. Shifted the user-hostile chair close. I didn't say any more and neither did she. I held her hand until it warmed in mine, and Skye fell asleep. I kept holding her hand until my shoulder ached.

I left when the nurse showed up with Skye's lunch. I was too brainspun for school, so I drifted home. Once there I couldn't get settled. It was like one part of my head was screwed in way too tight, and the other, way too loose. I did what repressed, socially incompetent adolescent males do. I booted up the hard drive.

I made a chart. I like charts. Graphs. Equations. I didn't have a clue what to put in the chart. I'd flow-chart until I got a pattern.

What I am: Low key. Lowest of keys. Music no one hears. Man of few opinions. Dull. On a treadmill going nowhere.

The last made me think. Yeah, that was it. Until lately, I was a creature of routine. Never going forward. I woke, I went to school, I hated it, I came home, I went to sleep.

And I started over again. No goal. No purpose. Just passing time until college.

What was Skye? I had a goal with her. Sex. Then to "save" her. She was frightening. Unpredictable. She was screwing with my head. My life. But she wasn't boring. She made me furious. She made my blood pound.

I pulled my fingers from the keys. Skye was my razor. She caused me pain, but the pain woke me up, proved I was alive.

Skye didn't want me to kill anyone. She knew enough about me to realize I wasn't the type to go cowboy. She needed reassurance and I had been stupid and scared. Heavy on the stupid. Shit, heavy on the scared.

She was screwy in big, bad ways, but she needed help. And there I went again. She needed me. She needs me. Needs me. *Needsmeneedsmeneedsme*.

Skye had held my hand. She didn't yell at me for coming to the hospital.

I erased the random sentences. This couldn't be charted.

Jeremy

Jeremy breezed in while I was watching reruns of "Buffy the Vampire Slayer." Now there's a girl with conflicts.

"Mattman, what's the haps with the no-school thing?"

He whispered this as he juked and jived.

I led him up to my room. He had on a Rasta knit cap and baggy pants.

"My name is Matt, and you are . . .?"

"Don't be a dick. Man, why wasn't I born black?"

As least this craziness was amusing. "Mmmm, I think both your parents' being white could be a factor."

"The whole black thing is so me. I can get with it."

"Jeremy or Black Dude in Disguise or whatever, you spent the weekend with fifty guys that are so WASP that they have to fart through Ralph Lauren. The black thing is not you."

Maybe there was a twelve-step program for too much gangsta rap.

"But it's so cool. The language alone. Listen up." He scrunched his face into a constipated twitch and said with a Brit accent, "I am pissed. I am extremely pissed." More hand waving. "Now, listen to it this way." Bobbing and weaving, fingers jabbing at the air, he said, "I be pissed! I be righteous pissed!" He grinned. "See the diff?"

I sighed. "Jeremy, you're an American, white, lost boy. Get with the program."

Jeremy rolled his eyes toward the ceiling as if it would help him think. "Okay, but I'm keeping the cap." He morphed back into his Anglo self. "Where were you today? There's more news than you can use."

"Tired. Too much party, not enough sack time. And, if I'm thinking of making it to graduation, I have to skip a few days for my own mental well-being."

Like I hadn't spoken, Jeremy launched into his spiel. "The Phi Delts are seriously interested in you for early rush. Me, too, of course. That's why I thought I'd get the funk out of my system before I got blazered and boat-shoed for four years.

"Second, Ann Fields got narced on to the Tri Delts. She's been told, legacy or no, she can't boff three guys at one party." He grinned. "I guess two is the sorority's moral limit." Hand wagging. "She's not out, she's just on probation.

"Third, Ken got a call from some Pikes. His dad was a Pike in, like, an earlier century, and they want to meet him." He shook his head. "Pike instead of Phi Delt. I doubt it. Ummm, that's all the bigs.

"Extraneous news is that one of the X-Ray girls is preggars. Everybody is wondering if the baby will be born anorexic, too. Quarterback sprained his pinky while spanking the monkey—well, the spanking part is purely speculation on my part, but I'm reporting it as fact to others, and Gothgirl tried to off herself."

Neutral, I told myself. Stay. Very. Cool. "Sprained his pinky?" I finally said.

Skye

I ditched school Tuesday. I wouldn't have to explain my school absence to my parents. They left in their separate cars to their separate jobs before me and didn't get home until after I did. And unless my failure to attend class was in double digits on the report card, I wouldn't have to tell them shit. They wouldn't ask. My parents are not uncaring, but they are busy. Unless I'm bleeding from the eyes, I don't draw filial attention. Easy for them. Good for me.

So I slept late, then drove to the hospital around noon. I pushed into Skye's room—and nobody home. Not nobody home, like, out for a minute and coming back. This was nobody home, as in, cleared out and sanitized.

"Are you a relative?" Monika, with a K, asked. What was it with the hospital types and their perky names?

"No, a good friend. Where is she?"

"I can't give you any information unless you are a relative."

"I am not asking to see her chart. I just want to know if she's in this hospital. Has she been released?" More likely, Skye had hit the wind.

"I'm sorry, I can't—"

"Right." I snapped the word off like I'd bitten a dangling hangnail. "I'm not from the right gene pool." I turned to leave, then whirled and did something I'd never done before. I made myself memorable.

"And, MoniKa, learn to spell your fucking name."

I stormed out.

I got in the car and cruised around, trying to cool down. Matt Lathrop had just been rude to someone who didn't deserve it.

I turned up the radio, drove a little saner, and worked to use my head for something other than counterweight for my feet.

Of course, Skye was still in the hospital. Misspelled Monica would have told me if she had been released. The only reason to insist on patient confidentiality was if Skye was there. Tracking on that scent, I figured Skye was moved to a lockdown unit. She must be doing in-house therapy or she had gone freakshow on them. How much more freaked could she get?

I almost smiled at that thought. With Skye, there was always the next level of crazy.

I couldn't just flap around, not knowing what was happening. I couldn't go see her parents or even call. Skye let me visit her. But she had been drifting in the ether and we were alone. A face-to-face with her parents would send her into overdrive.

Matt couldn't call, but Bob the tutor could.

Where could this go wrong? Caller ID could be a

problem. Fine, pay phone. I flipped the idea around, looking for wormholes. None was evident. Great. Bob the tutor would call tonight.

The Colbys

"Hello?"

"Hello, is this Mr. Colby?"

"Yes, who's calling, please?"

"Mr. Colby, my name is Bob and I—"

"Are you Skye's tutor?"

Somehow I hadn't expected that. Skye's parents—her father, particularly—being so tuned in to the details of her life.

"Yes. I haven't seen her at school, so I picked up some assignments. I guess she's got the flu that's going around?" I sounded sincere—even to myself. Maybe lying to yourself isn't as hard as it sounds.

"No, I mean—I don't know what I mean." Mr. Colby's voice cracked, like a sob had crept up his throat. He made the "give me a minute" clearing sound, then, "No, Skye doesn't have the flu. She's in the hospital and will be for two or three weeks. You might as well hear it from me, Bob. I'm sure the rumor mill will have the story soon anyway." He cleared his throat again. "Skye took an overdose of pills. She's doing a kind of rehab and lots of therapy."

"Oh," I said. Let him talk, I said to myself. Let him talk.

"Yes, um, Skye has problems and the doctor thinks she needs to stay there for treatment rather than do out-patient work." He sounded like he was reading from a monitor.

He didn't say any more.

"I understand. I guess that means she can't have visitors?"

"No," Mr. Colby said. Just that one word sounded sad and bleak. "No, not even me or Skye's stepmother."

Stepmother.

Dead air. I couldn't think.

"But," Mr. Colby took over, "I'll ask the doctor about homework. It might be good if she could keep up with her studies."

"Okay, I can bring the assignments by, or e-mail them to you if that's easier."

"E-mail?" Mr. Colby sounded puzzled. "Oh, yes, you kids do that a lot, don't you? I must sound prehistoric, but we don't have a computer."

No computer? But Skye e-mailed me. She had to be home when she IM'ed me—she came straight home to watch Lisa. Skye had told me that.

"No problem, Mr. Colby. I'll just leave the stuff on your porch if you're not there when I come by."

"Actually, my wife and I would like to meet you. To thank you for your help."

I hesitated a minute. But my curiosity trumped my

fear of Skye's disapproval. "That would be great. I can come by tomorrow at six or so. Will that interrupt anything?"

"That's fine," Mr. Colby said. "We'll see you then."

Promptly at six, looking like a Boy Scout and toting a history text and a folder of old assignments, I stood, straight-backed and tutorly, at the Colbys' door. A slim woman answered my knock. Another surprise. This woman was never a crack whore. Not in my TV-fueled experience anyway. She was young, probably not thirty, and her skin made its own sunlight. Short, tousled hair, open grin, snappy eyes that appraised, approved, and invited me in.

"Bob?"

"Yes, Mrs. Colby?"

"Tammy."

Tammy. Tammy who looked like she could tote a surfboard and ride goofy foot on the crest of a ten-footer. A golden one who could never provide DNA for the dark Skye.

"Come in. We've looked forward to meeting you."

"Lex, come meet Bob." She ushered me into the family room. "Have a seat."

Lex appeared then. Older than his wife by about fifteen years, he was blond and all hale and hearty and straight-toothed charm. He shook my hand. "Bob. You're the first friend of Skye's that didn't look dressed for Halloween."

I felt dressed for Halloween. I wore the Dockers that my mother bought a year ago, store creases still sharp. And an I'm-too-prep-to-live pinstriped shirt that also resided in the back of the closet. I looked like an Eddie Bauer refugee.

Lex gestured for me to sit. I sat. Placed the book and papers on the coffee table. "I didn't know if Skye had her book, so I brought one."

"Thanks."

I asked about Skye and got polite answers that she was not as combative with her therapist as on previous occasions. They hoped for a positive result this time.

"She's a deeply troubled girl," Lex said. "I want so much for her to be happy. I had custody, but her mother took her and ran off, you know, when Skye was three. I got her back when she was five, but . . ." He looked close to tears. "She seemed fine for so long. Then we moved here and Tammy and I married and . . ."

"Lex," Tammy said gently. "Bob, doesn't need to sort through our baggage."

Lex straightened. "I know, sorry, Bob."

"Lex rips himself up over Skye," Tammy said. "I worry, too. But, I'm a little more objective." She smiled. "We're glad you've been helping her."

I know that pervs don't come with a sign on their forehead—"KEEP AWAY, I MOLEST"—but if this guy had ever touched Skye, I'd eat a chocolate-covered cat turd.

"I'll admit I'm a little confused," I said. "I send Skye assignments by e-mail and she e-mails me her questions."

Lex looked puzzled.

"She said she stays home a lot, taking care of her little sister."

"Sister?" Tammy and Lex exchanged glances, looking to each other for a clue.

"We just told Skye that Tammy is pregnant. We don't know if it's a girl. And"—he shook his head—"this doesn't make sense."

"I meant Lisa." Had they already put the poor kid out of their minds?

Tammy's confusion cleared immediately. "Lisa." She looked down and sighed. "Lisa isn't Skye's sister."

I stared at them. Then anger surged through me. At Skye. How many times would she lie to me? And how many times would I believe her?

I drove home through the fog—thicker in my head than on the road. Lisa was not in a state horror house. She was Tammy's niece. Tammy kept her on Saturdays so her sister could run errands and get a little alone time. As for Skye, she tended to be courteous but remote with Lisa. She certainly didn't baby-sit.

Lex knew that Skye spent a lot of time at a local cybercafé. He assumed that's where she got and sent e-mail.

I was the guy who didn't trust, but when Skye said she stayed home and watched Lisa, I didn't question it. But I knew Skye was one of the hang-out people. I'd seen her. Hell, I'd even seen her at WIRED, clanking and tapping at a terminal. How stupid was I?

The fog cleared a bit. I had an answer. Skye didn't want me to kill anyone. Skye needed drama in her life, so she wrote her own script. I'd proved myself a willing audience. And now Tammy was pregnant. Skye was afraid the new baby would steal her place in her parents' life. She had lost her safety net. I knew how that felt.

I got home, microwaved a leftover that appeared to be soup, and took it to my room. I was too amped for homework.

I pulled up my program and sorted through my chart of lies, diversions, truths. Now that I was out of the Colbys' house, it occurred to me that I was a pushover. If nothing Skye told me was true—did she need me at all?

I scarfed the pseudosoup, then guzzled a Coke and tried to mellow. There was nothing I could do for three weeks or so. The Colbys said Skye would be in the hospital for at least that long.

I sighed. There I went again. Why did I believe them? Were they shipping her off to a state funny farm? Was she locked in the attic? Did they really not own a computer?

I called Ken. "Ken, I need a bit of your computer geekness."

"You may speak," he said.

"Can you look at an e-mail and find out where it came from?"

"More info."

"Right, if I forward you an e-mail someone sent me,

can you tell from all the bullshit in the header if it came from a personal account or from a public terminal?"

"Like a library or cybercafé?"

"That would be correct. Like that."

"Can do. Have done. Will do again."

"Great. All right, I'm deleting the actual post and just sending the cyber gook part." I hit Send.

I heard a nasal buzz. Ken was humming. Kind of atonal, but maybe the theme from "Gilligan's Island"?

"Got it," Ken said. "Give me a minute."

I heard Ken tapping keys. "What's with this? Trying to hack into someone's account for free service?"

"Can you do that?"

"I wish I could tell you," Ken said. "But then I'd have to . . . you know."

"Kill me. I know." Too much talk about killing lately.

"Okay, that was easy. This person paid for time at WIRED. It's not a home account."

"I thought it might be."

"Hmm, Matt. StormySkye? Please don't tell me you're hooked up with Gothgirl."

"Hooked up? Nope. But I did get a post from her or someone using her screen name. It was about school assignments. Wanting me to pick them up for her."

"Why would someone think you would do that for a crazy chick you hardly know?"

"That was my thought," I lied. To my own friend. Not my parents or a teacher—a person who counted.

"True."

"Maybe somebody wants to jerk me off. Figuring I'm so hard up, I'd scuttle around getting assignments because a girl was involved. I dunno."

"That makes a little sense," Ken said. "Not a lot, but a little."

"Forget it, Ken. It's a replay of when Scott Bayles told me he saw my wallet in the locker room. I still have the scar on my forehead from that one."

"Sixth grade," Ken said. "October. I remember."

I changed the subject. "So what's this about your dad being a Pike?"

"I so wish I was an orphan," Ken said.

I didn't respond.

"Dad was a Pike at some dink school and he thinks I should be one at UT."

"And what do you think?"

Ken sighed. "I will repeat, verbatim, something he said, and that should answer your question. 'Ken, son, back when I was a Pike, we were the happening fraternity. I mean, we had it goin' aaaawn!'"

I pictured Ken's dad, drawling out the word "on."

"Ken, it's official. You were adopted. That man cannot be your father."

"That would be my wish." Ken sighed. "I'm a pathetic loser, but Dad defies description."

We shot the shit a little longer; then I hung up.

I tapped into a search engine and typed a phrase Mr. Colby had used when he talked about Skye.

Loss of affect.

I followed links from one site to another. I read about teens who don't engage. A generation of observers rather than participants.

I'm not sure I found Skye there, but I might have found a shadow of myself.

Observer. I didn't engage in school or home. A non-participant? Taylor had called me reactive rather than active. That hadn't bothered me then. But it bothered me now. Screw the whoevers who thought they knew the whatevers. I could participate. I would participate.

Taylor

Enough with Skye and her lies. Skye didn't need me.

I would have a sane girl, one who could walk into a frat house on my arm. One who didn't drive me crazy with lies. One I didn't have to hide. One I didn't have to box away from other boxes.

And I would be active. I would participate until I swept her off her feet. I got in my car and headed to Taylor's.

She lived in a *Gone with the Wind* kind of house on a lake. Spanish moss hung from huge oaks. A porch light glowed, illuminating two figures. Taylor was in major make-out mode with someone who appeared to have more muscles in his neck than I had in my shoulders. I guess I sat there watching a little too long. Taylor leaned to get a look, saw me, and waved. I goosed the accelerator and shot away. Very cool behavior—if you are in fourth grade.

My phone was ringing when I walked into my room.

"What?" Not only cool, but also so socially correct.

"Matt?"

"Yes, Taylor." I hung my head and toed the nap of the

carpet. "That was me. But I was not stalking you. Well, I was only semi-stalking you. Forget it."

"I waved. Why didn't you come up to the porch? I wanted you to meet Rick."

Didn't this poised, primo girl get it? Couldn't she see?

"Rick?"

"Matt . . ." Taylor drifted off. "Oh . . . You thought . . . I . . . uh . . ."

I flipped from sheepish to pissed. "What's the deal with you, anyway? You talk to me, you come get me at the beach, you button me up at a frat party, but you don't get it."

"Matt, Rick's a sophomore at A and M. I've been dating him for over a year. Everybody knows that."

I didn't.

"I wasn't leading you on. Rick comes down two weekends a month to see me. This isn't a big secret."

I didn't know what to say. I had never seen past Taylor's glow. I was incredibly stupid. Not only no participant, I was shit for an observer.

Matt

Days passed and I ran on my hamster wheel. Went to school, stayed low, low enough that Ken and Jeremy told me I needed a laxative to shake me loose. Actually, Jeremy suggested the laxative; Ken thought I needed a jolt from those electric paddles doctors wield in TV emergency rooms.

My grades went south, I knew the plot of every lame sitcom on cable reruns, I lost weight and slept as much as I could manage. If I was alert, I tended to think. That wasn't good.

Taylor tried to talk to me at school and called me at home a couple of times, but I was monosyllabic boy. She told me to call her when I got over myself. Like that would happen. My drab existence faded to a paler shade of gray and I drifted.

Until Skye came back.

Skye

I saw her in the hall on Monday. She breezed past me and everyone else without a hint of acknowledgment. She looked good. Distant but good. Her hair was still spiky and tousled, but it looked like someone had evened out the hacked parts. She seemed rested, and there was a hint of color skimming along her cheekbones. She wore black silky tights and a shirt that almost covered a short skirt. A tie was knotted against her skin inside the collar of the shirt and she wore a short leather vest over the whole thing. Sexy as homemade sin. Her mood was unreadable. But my track record for perception . . . well, the less said.

Gossip surrounded Skye like a swarm of stinging mosquitoes. She had run away and was living with Satanists. She had AIDS and had tried to end it. She had a miscarriage. Twins. She had been in jail, not the hospital. She had been kidnapped by a trick gone bad.

I was certain that Skye had leaked most of the stories.

It was my first interesting day in three weeks.

Park. 9.

I wondered why Skye's parents, if their concern hadn't been an act, weren't keeping a leash on her. How could a girl toting these problems and fresh off the funny farm be allowed to haunt cybercafés after school and wander the park at night? But by now, I knew better than to ask.

I blazed through my calculus homework, then looked for a paper on the Internet about theater in the Dark Ages, so I could lift the important parts. I didn't have to worry about plagiarism. There weren't any papers to find. I figure that was evidence enough that there wasn't enough theater in the Dark Ages to count for anything. Great. Now I'd have to do real research. Why don't teachers get it? If it's not on the Web to be copied, it's not important. Case closed.

I slopped together some Hamburger Helper for Dad and me, and watched a few reruns of Buffy to set the tone for my meeting with Skye. While Buffy was trying to sort out why instead of killing a vampire, she was boffing one, Katy plopped down on the couch with a plate of couscous and a penetrating stare.

Not good. Ever.

Katy

"Matt."

"Yep, that would be me."

"So . . ."

I winced. If Katy's opener was "so," it suggested a comfort level associated with drowning kittens.

"I—um—finally figured something out. Or think I did."

"And is this a good thing? You don't look like it's a good thing," I said.

"Well, the other night, well, I mean, you know, weeks ago, I wasn't all that helpful," Katy said.

I put up my hands. "Don't go there. You were right. I shouldn't have dumped that on you. And it's okay. That's worked itself out."

"It has? That's great."

"Yeah. Great," I said.

"That's not all I wanted to say," Katy said.

I hit the remote. This was officially a conversation. One thing at a time.

"Go," I said.

"Hmmm, I keep, like, rerunning the conversation and something kept bothering me and it took me a while, but I finally realized what it was."

I waited.

"You always said 'this person.'"

"Right. I told you I wouldn't give you a name."

"I know, but you didn't give something else," Katy said. "You never said if it was a he or a she."

I looked at Katy, waiting. But she didn't say anything else. What did she want? I didn't . . . oh, shit.

"Katy."

She placed her couscous with careful precision on the coffee table. "Matt. I get it now. And it's fine. I don't know why you didn't think you could tell me. I don't know why I didn't figure it out before." Katy was falling all over herself to talk. Words rushing out of her like water from a burst pipe.

"You never go to, like, the school dances or homecoming or anything like that. You don't date at all. And now you're suddenly meeting somebody at odd hours and you don't let anybody know who or where. And then we have this weird talk and it's all 'this person'"—she gestured with her left hand, "and 'this person'"—whirled her right hand in the air.

"If it was a she you would have said 'she' somewhere in the conversation. Wouldn't you?" Katy took a breath and plunged ahead before I could get a word in.

"So, you're gay. And that's totally, completely fine. Well, with me. Dad will freak, but we'll make him behave, and I want to meet your—uh, boyfriend. Or what do you call him? I—ummmph!"

I clamped my hand over Katy's mouth. I didn't know how else to stop her. "I'll let go if you promise not to talk." She nodded, her eyes huge.

I let go. "Katy, thanks for the support, but I'm not gay." She sputtered. "No talking. I don't date because girls do not want to be seen with me. I like girls. They do not return the feeling. I am seeing a girl. I don't bring her around for two reasons. One, because she lies, drinks, takes drugs, and steals. Two, because even she doesn't want to be seen with me."

"Can I talk now?"

"Just a little."

"Why do you see her?"

That stopped me. I looked at Katy for several long, long seconds and then I said the only thing that seemed true. "Excitement."

I paused, thinking. "And because she's everything I'm not."

Katy sat for a minute. And then she said something that scared me.

"You know, I think I get that."

Skye

She was there when I arrived. Sitting steady on the table, the full moon caressing her features. Face scrubbed, hair tousled but not spiked, the skull earring dancing from her lobe. She appeared calm. Sane.

The vulnerable heart-squeeze smile greeted my hello. Things were crazy. My boxes wouldn't stay straight. Data kept jumping from one file into another. Or rather, the files kept turning into people or the data into emotions or—I don't know, I was losing it.

I sat next to her, and she nuzzled into my shoulder. I kissed her hair and pulled her snug into my side.

"I'm disappointed," I said.

"How so?"

"I hoped you'd get out of the bin and have those kinky cloth handcuffs."

She laughed, soft and low down, in amusement and gratitude that I had broken the ice. That I had accepted Skye with all her frailties.

"You're a perv."

"Guilty," I said. I set the skull swaying with my tongue. "Cuff me, officer."

Skye twisted in my arms to face me, and traced my

features with her fingertips. "I missed you." She sighed and snugged against my chest. "You came to the hospital?"

It was a question. I guess knowing what parts of those days were real was tricky.

"I came to the hospital."

"You held my hand. And you didn't let go for a long time."

I remembered the ache in my arm and shoulder. "I didn't let go until they ran me off."

"I'd die without you."

Was that commitment?

Intention?

I tipped her face up so she looked at me. "No use of the word die or any of its synonyms or derivatives."

Her smile this time was tired. "Yes, Professor."

We sat in the park for an hour, listening to the crickets and the full-throated bullfrogs, talking easily. She told me about the three weeks in Loonville, mostly about the other patients. I told her the rumors concerning her hiatus. She told me which stories she had planted. All of them.

We kissed and snuggled. We were real.

I drove her home, not asking how she had gotten to the park in the first place, and let her off at the end of her street, per her demand. After she stepped out and closed the car door, she motioned me to put the window down.

"Thanks for everything." She paused and backed away. "Bob."

She drifted down the street without another word or even a backward glance.

Skye. Skye. Skye.

I was in a free fall and enjoying it. Skye didn't poke any hornets' nests at school. I don't know if she was taking mood-altering drugs, but her mood was definitely altered. So was mine. Well, I finally had a mood. I don't think neutral counts and that's all I previously knew. Now, I found myself grinning at odd moments, day-dreaming my life. Christmas break nosed into the lineup and I was meeting Skye at the beach house often.

I'd usually get there in the afternoon, and sometimes we cooked. Cook, for me, means boiling spaghetti and pouring sauce out of a jar, but Skye had managed a bottle of red and some candles. First on our agenda was always sex, then food. We sat, half dressed, draped in blankets in the dim house, our features highlighted by the flicker of the candle flame.

It was good. Hell, it was great.

But not for long.

We met the day after Christmas, and Skye had a little DVD player. The personal kind, like they rent in airports.

"Sweet," I said. "These things are expensive."

Skye didn't say anything. She handed me a stack of DVDs.

"Santa was good to you," I said. But I knew.

I knew.

Her eyes, which had been soft and sane for a week or two, were blank again.

"Sure," she said. "Santa."

I watched the DVDs and ate canned chili that night, but the glow stayed in the candles. Skye was aggressive rather than loving—okay, I'll admit it, rather than needy, and sex didn't quite work.

There was a blowout frat party that Jeremy assumed I would be attending. Until now I was going to spend the weekend with Skye. But she was shoplifting, lying . . .

I returned the favor.

"Skye, I'm going out of town with my parents for New Year's. To see my grandparents."

She let the silence deepen, grow heavy.

"I thought your grandparents came down Christmas Eve."

Busted.

"Skye, a lot of people have two sets of grandparents. I'm one of those double-geezered kids."

"Sure."

"I'll call or e you as soon as I get back."

"Sure." She shrugged. "That's fine."

Ex-friends

I went to Austin with Ken and Jeremy. New Year's Eve with the frat boys.

Somehow, nothing was hanging together now. When I was with saneSkye the world was full of color and texture. WeirdSkye world was full of lost light. And frat world was tepid and flat. I had the greener-grass syndrome. Big and bad.

And it showed.

"Mattman, what's with you lately?" I bumped along in the backseat of Ken's Pathfinder. Jeremy spoke to me from shotgun position.

"Nothing's with me. I did the whole moderation thing. I was a good, good lad."

"No, not the boozing. You're all—you know, emo."

"I'm a tall, long-necked bird with a tiny head?"

Ken chortled. "That's, like, emu."

"Emo, dude. Emotional to the fifth power."

"Jeremy, I've never been emo. Not even to the first power."

"Okay, emo isn't quite right. But you're all moody and muse-y, ya know?"

I opted for the generic answer. I shrugged. That one shoulder hike, release thing.

"You're never around." His voice went sing-songy. "Ya don't call, ya don't write. . . ."

If he'd been female, he would have been accused of jealousy. "Jeremy, when did we get engaged?"

Ken chortled again. The sound was a snort that sounded like he was saying "chort, chort, chort," back in his throat, followed by a clucking noise, like he was learning to say his l's. I couldn't decide if it was annoying or gag-worthy.

Jeremy cocked his wrist and batted my knee. "You silly." Then he presto-change-oed into interrogator mode. "Give it up. You got something going on the side?"

His tone surprised me. It wasn't friendly, it was accusatory.

Ken didn't chortle now. He flashed me a sideways glance that broadcasted his guilt.

"What do you mean, Jeremy?"

"A rumor is floating that you're boinking Gothgirl." His voice had an edge when he said "boinking." Of what? God, he was jealous I might be having sex.

Neutralneutralneutral, I told my face.

I looked at the back of Ken's head. "Good to meet you Rumor, my name is Matt."

The back of Ken's neck got the red creeps.

"Tell me you're not involved with that freak," Jeremy demanded.

"Jeremy, I don't need your approval for my boinking or involvements or anything else."

"Dude, you can screw over your chances of being a Phi Delt if you—"

I didn't let him finish. "Are you threatening me, Jeremy? Are you really telling me that if I don't get permission from you, don't date someone you approve, your brother will goober me with the frat? Are you saying that to me, Jeremy? Me, one of the two friends you have?"

And I saw something in Jeremy I had never seen. Never expected to see. He looked just like one of the jocks when a loser appeared on the radar. He had that "how dare you" thing going on. Geez, hand even the lowest-ranking nerd a whiff of power and it corrupted him. He forgot I was the fourth-grader who put ice on his face after Skip Lauer pushed it into an anthill and then sat on him.

We drove the rest of the way in silence.

Skye

I took a major chance and called Skye's house when I got home. Her stepmom answered. Pulling my Bob-the-tutor persona out of my ass, I asked for Skye.

"She's not here, Bob." Tammy paused. "We've tried to limit Skye's comings and goings, but she slips out when we don't have her in sight. She told me she was doing homework in her room. I looked in on her a few minutes ago and she was gone. We don't know how she's getting past the security system."

I thanked her and hung up. So, if she was stepmother and not stepmonster, and if she was telling the truth, Tammy and Lex tried to keep Skye safe. And failed as miserably as I did.

I sent an e-mail:

Call.

She didn't call, but she e'd me.

Since when have your grandparents been Phi Delts? Asshole.

I guess it didn't surprise me that she knew I'd lied. The surprise was that she had details. I didn't know what to do with that.

Monday, I arrived at school and strolled past Skye's locker. A bumper sticker was pasted to it—a serious infraction of school rules concerning respect for property. "NUKE THE UNBORN GAY BABY WHALES FOR JESUS." While I knew this meant a return to Skye's destructo phase, I had to admire her skill at being an equal-opportunity offender. Word from Ken's sister was that the principal had already clocked Skye for the offense and the offensiveness. He was recommending expulsion. Skye was suspended until a hearing with the school board.

Not good. Skye went ballistic if authority figures did power trips on her. This would get ugly quick.

From the library's computer, I e-mailed her several groveling apologies. I was spending lunch there, now that my friends had become ex.

Katy

Katy had her fourteenth birthday bash Saturday night. Mom somehow turned the place into a 70s disco with a flashing floor and racks of bell-bottoms and hip-hugger costumes for the attendees. The giggle meter topped out. Katy even managed to drape me with a pink feather boa, and I stumbled around the dance floor with her, once—there are limits to brotherly devotion. If I had known what Monday's mail would bring, I would have worn the white polyester suit and danced with every girl there.

Matt the Liar

Monday, Skye still wasn't back in class and I hadn't heard from her in days, so I skipped my Coke float again and headed for my room to check my e-mail. Katy sat on my bed. She held a letter and she was crying.

"Katy?"

She said nothing. She sobbed so hard I wasn't sure she could breathe.

"Katy?" I said again. The air was wrong. All wrong.

"Go look in my room," she choked out.

In her room sat wired and ready to cybersurf, a top-of-the-line iMac. Huge honking monitor and newest, speed-of-light OS flashing its logo in all its multipixeled glory.

Nobody Katy knew would send a gift like this. And why would it make Katy cry like her heart . . . Something bitter flowed into my mouth. I hadn't been watching closely enough.

It would all come out now. And I wasn't going to be the hero. I stood there, knowing I should go back to her, but dreading it. It would be a dead man's walk.

Why had I been so concerned with myself and

missed the clues? Morgan didn't have a stalker. Katy was the prey. And I hadn't kept her safe.

I gathered up the little courage I had, and went to Katy. I sat on the bed next to her.

"Tell me," I said.

She knuckled her eyes, swiped her nose, and sighed hard a few times. "The doorbell rang. A delivery guy from the computer store was there. I saw his van—had the store's logo. I even asked to see the delivery papers."

I put my arm around her. "It's fine. You're always cool about strangers. Go ahead."

She nodded. Fast, then rubbed her eyes again. "He handed me this letter." She thrust the envelope into my lap. Typed on the thick cream-colored paper was: "To Katy, You'll need this for high school. From, Your Father."

If only I had been home before Katy. I knew Katy was getting my computer at graduation. Dad would never send her this. And if he did, the card would read "Katy-did." I would have sensed the wrong, but Katy . . . I had protected Katy right into the biggest hurt of her life.

"So, another guy comes out of the van with that computer, big bow on it, not even in the box. I let him in and he put it in my room. I sign the receipt and off they go. I thought Dad had gone, like, old-fart crazy or something. I mean, how long had I bugged him for a computer?"

I closed my eyes and nodded. I felt so tired. I didn't have to look over my shoulder anymore. The traffic accident was here.

"Then I read this." She shoved the letter at me.

"You're not going to believe it."

I picked it up. Two pages. Typed. Typed for god's sakes. Did he have his secretary do it? I scanned the sheets. I knew what was there.

I handed the pages back. They shook, tips fluttering. I stood and paced, getting faster, steps lengthening, circles tightening in the small room.

"That miserable piece of . . . !"

Katy stared.

I whirled and snatched a notebook, slamming it on the desktop, a two-hand grip, shoulders and back into it, wishing I was pounding the sleazebag's face.

"If I could get my hands on him, I swear I'd rip his throat out, I'd—"

And then I saw realization cross Katy's features.

"You knew," she whispered. Like it was something so ugly it couldn't be said aloud.

I didn't say anything. I understood now what dead silence really means.

Her eyes left mine and drifted down. Slow. Shifting, landing here, then there, not seeing, then down again.

"It's true." All the Katyness seemed to leak out of her, leaving someone I'd never met, a Katyghost. "And you knew it."

Tears stung my eyes. I rocked slightly. Back and forth. I had been losing my grip on a lot of things lately, but this—it would never be the same for us again.

Never.

She stood up. Stronger now. Still not my Katy, but filled with anger, rather than hollow. "You. Knew."

I still didn't answer. We let the silence swamp us.

Katy took a deep breath. "How long?" It was a demand.

I sighed and sat on the bed. "Since I was ten."

Katy staggered as if I had slapped her.

She stepped back. Away from me.

I couldn't look at her, but I could hear her ragged, angry breath.

"The one thing I always had. The thing I always trusted." She stopped. "Was you."

"Katy, I—"

"You knew they were lying to me. It was up to you to make sure I had one person to trust. Or am I only half as important?"

She turned her back on me and strode to the door.

"Katy, let me explain," I said.

"Don't," she said. "Don't talk to me. There's nothing you can say that I can ever believe."

I sat slumped in the chair for who knows how long. I heard Dad come in. I heard Katy go into his office and close the door. I could feel little sympathy for him. Sure, he's kept the family together and I guess he'd forgiven Mom, even though we were a family of strangers. I sighed. Complete. We were now a family of complete strangers.

I wandered to the bed and crashed. I stared at the ceiling like it would give me answers. The room darkened. That was fine. Mom came in, shouting hellos that went unanswered. I heard her go to Katy's room. Katy told her to go away. Mom tapped on my door. I told her to talk to Dad. She did.

Mom came back to my room. "Matt?"

"Mom, you and Dad have to take care of Katy now. I'm fine."

"But we need to talk."

"Sure, but not now."

Mom came to the bed and smoothed my hair. "This is such a mess and it's all my fault. I wanted us all to talk together but . . ."

Knife to heart. Twist hard. "But Katy won't talk if I'm anywhere close, right?"

Mom's silence was the answer.

"Go, Mom, Katy needs you."

She went.

I assessed my world. My little sister would no longer look to me as her hero. Or even as her real brother. And I deserved it. My parents had put me in this position. Ken had ratted me out to Jeremy. Jeremy would make sure my dream of frat man would never happen. Taylor Banks knew I was pathetic. I could hear the sobs and shouts of family meltdown swirling around me. Is this how Skye lived?

Abandoned?

Or is it betrayed?

Certalnly—lost.

My world of boxes was a house of cards. Everything had collapsed and I couldn't control anything. I was alone in this mess.

I got up and typed out an e-mail.

Have to see U. Please. Call.

I heard Mom, Dad, and Katy, voices rising, then lowering, stopping, starting, rushing, and slowing. I flung myself back on the bed, put the phone on my stomach and the pillow over my face.

—

The phone rang at nine. Skye. I could hear the roar of traffic in the background. She was at a pay phone. "Meet me at the beach at ten."

She hung up.

Skye

The moon, winding down, still managed to turn the lapping wave foam into neon snakes on the dark water. The beach house was dark, but the porch light was on and I could make out Skye's silhouette near the water. She was pacing hard, staggering a bit when she pivoted to change direction.

"Hey, are you going to hit me?" I asked. "Or forgive me?"

"That depends."

Her tone was flat. The words clipped and hard. I was going to have to work for forgiveness. But I wanted it. I didn't have anyone else.

I moved toward her and smelled the liquor on her breath. She held up both hands to keep me at bay. "No touchy-feelies."

"That's fair."

She paced more furiously, then wheeled on me. "It's time to piss or get off the pot."

"What's that mean?"

"My parents. It's time."

"Time? For what?" Before the words sounded, I

knew. "No, no way. I can't. I won't. Skye, you don't want me to. You're mad and you're testing me and—"

"Shut up. And don't tell me what I want."

I walked away and sat on a porch step. Skye stood tense and stiff, then pounded across the sand and glared down at me.

I was tired. Tired of tonight. Tired of people pounding on me with words. "Skye, I don't know if you were molested. If so, I hurt for you, but I don't think Lex ever touched you like that."

"And what makes you the fucking swami?"

"Because you lied about Lisa. She's not your sister. You don't stay home and take care of her. And if you lied to me about that, you probably lied about Lex."

"I guess you're the expert on lying."

Yeah, I guess so.

"And you're pissed because Tammy is pregnant. You think you'll lose what little place you have in your family."

"Shut up!"

When I looked at her, she was—smirking.

"You're so incredibly stupid. And you were so easy. If you weren't so pitiful, you'd be amusing."

There was only hatred in her now. I came here to tell her that I needed, wanted comfort and solace. Wanted her. But now I knew we were over. She was too much, too soon, and I was too little, too late.

We were finally done.

▬

She cocked out one hip and placed her fist on it. "Let's talk about your parents."

Huh? What was this switch?

"What about them?"

"Don't you get that they've abused you with neglect? You're a piece of furniture for them."

"That's not true. They're just—"

"Busy people. You told me. Face it, moron. Your mother and father are a TV and a VCR. That's who spends time with you. That's where you learn things. Your parents don't give a rat's ass. They're always gone. They don't know the first thing about you."

I sighed. "Skye, you don't know the first thing about my family."

"Some people are prey, some predators. Which are you, Matt?"

I pulled my eyelashes.

Enough.

Enough.

Enough.

My anger rose. Maybe it was leftover anger at my ruined family. Maybe it was anger at myself for not protecting Katy. Maybe the anger was at Skye because she was a manipulative bitch.

"I don't have time for this. We're done. You hate me. I deserve it. But you don't need your parents dead. You don't need to escape Lex; you don't need to save Lisa. It's all a crock."

Skye leaned in, spewing her venom into my face.

"So, even if they pay you no more attention than a hangnail, you defend them. I guess that means you love them or something?"

There was no way I could answer that question. I loved them, I was angry with them, I wanted to . . . I don't know what I wanted.

I ran my fingers through my hair, massaging my scalp. "This is getting us nowhere. I'm leaving."

Her smile was evil. The porch light caught her teeth and they glistened. "I know someone you do love. Someone you want to protect." She jerked something out of her coat pocket and tossed it into my lap.

It was several pieces of folded paper. I opened them and turned to the light. Digital photos, printed on copy paper. They were indistinct because they were taken in low light. They must have been taken two weeks ago. When I was in Austin.

It had been a full moon then. The moon showed clearly through the blinds in my sister's bedroom. The shots were from the doorway of my sister's room. All the photographs were of Katy sleeping.

I knew what rage was in that moment.

"You crazy bitch!"

"Now you know that I can get at her whenever, wherever I please."

The blood pounded behind my eyes.

"You see, Matt, I'm six months shy of eighteen. And they are talking about a will. A will that puts money in trust. A trust I can't get to until I'm thirty-five."

She smiled again. I hated that smile. I hated her.

"Thirty-five? I don't think so. Then this baby thing comes and I had to put the plan into high gear. If they die now, before they get around to that will, I inherit. I'm too old to go back in foster care. The state will be glad to declare me an emancipated minor and the money's mine. The house, the car—everything."

"Big deal. You can go to college. You don't need to—"

"Sure, four more years of being under their thumb. No. School and I don't get along."

"So you want me to kill them?"

She shrugged. "They're in my way."

"Do it yourself. Find someone else. Kill yourself instead."

"Nope. If you don't kill my parents"—she pointed to the photos—"then I kill your precious little sister."

I couldn't process this. I heard the words, but—

"Don't you see it's why I picked you out?" She smiled again. No, smirked. Nothing that ugly could be called a smile. "You're a nobody. Who would connect us? And you won't let me hurt your little Katy."

She staggered a little, unbalanced. "Why do you think I told you Lisa was my sister? Don't you know I set up the thing with Squirrel at the rave with those skinny girls?" She laughed. Freak-show, circus-lady laugh. "I tricked you. Like someone can kick a drug dealer in the head and walk away for real?"

She pointed to the pictures. "Protecting the sister thing—I think you need a little therapy, ya know?"

I stood, the papers fluttering in the breeze. Staring. Finally, I found my voice. "Fuck you. I'm going to the police. Right now." I turned toward my car.

"I don't think so." Her voice was flat.

I heard a click. Turned back. She held a pistol.

"Loaded," she said.

I couldn't say a word. The dark hole of the barrel in my face was more terrifying than I could ever have imagined.

"Now, I don't want to do this. But, see, you forced me into it."

Her tone morphed from flat to angry. "You thought you could play mattress monkey with me and not have to pay?"

She had played me like a big, stupid fish. Hooked me with attention, set the hook with sex, reeled me in, then when I threatened to snap the line, she'd let me run, tiring myself out, fighting myself. Now, she was ready to gaff me.

The anger surged over the terror. I screamed at her.

"Then kill me, Skye. Kill the person who loved you. The person that held your hand in the hospital."

Something played across her features. I couldn't read it.

But it was hesitation.

And I used it.

"I held your hand in the hospital and I didn't let go."

She turned the gun and placed it against her temple. Wavered.

She turned it back to me.

Back to herself.

Playing a demented game.

No smiles now. No smirks.

She turned the gun back to me.

I took a step toward her, leaned in, and spoke, no, almost growled. "You're like those evil flying monkeys. The only reason you exist is to swoop down, rip things apart, and scatter the pieces."

I stepped back. "The money won't do you any good. Because you're no good to anyone—not even to yourself."

I saw it wound her, and her real Skyeness entered me. I wanted to hurt her. I liked it.

She steadied the gun. Gathered herself. Forced the flame back into her eyes.

"Make your choice. Me, you, my parents, your sister. Who do you want dead the most?" She put the barrel once more to her temple.

Back to me.

Back to her.

Now I knew there were levels of rage. And I had just reached critical mass.

She moved the gun back to me. I stared into the barrel. I stared into those dark eyes.

And I hated.

She moved the barrel back to her own temple.

Who did I want dead the most?

I didn't look away when I spoke.

"You," I said.

I think the shine in her eyes was tears.

And her lips moved.

But I'm not certain what she said.

I couldn't hear over the roar of the gun.